This book is dedicated to my granddaughter Sa'Kari Lynn. She sparked my creativity when I felt as if there was none there. In addition, I am forever grateful for my mother Linda, my children Khaalidah, Kymaani, Tylan and Taj, they inspire me and give me reason to chase my dreams. I also want to thank my love, Erik, for constantly pushing me and supporting all that is me. I love you all. A special thank you to the readers who have supported me from the beginning, and I welcome and appreciate all of my new readers, it means everything.

Chapter 1

"Troy, I don't think that looks good right there at all."

"No, I don't think it looks bad, but hey what do I know? Where would you like it Queen Naomi?"

He bows his head playfully waiting for his wife to tell him where to place the huge floor vase.

Naomi rolls her big brown eyes and motions for him to place it by the doorway.

"Baby I can't believe we are homeowners, can you? Seems like yesterday we were just in a little one-bedroom apartment fighting for closet space."

Troy plops down on the couch admiring their home.

"Well, it was just yesterday silly, we just moved in here today." Naomi shakes her head.

"And yeah, now we can fight over both fitting in the little kitchen and probably these ghetto neighbors." She walks off into the kitchen.

Troy gets up to follow.

"Damn baby, I mean I know it's not a dream home per se, but it's OURS, we're still young, give it some time, you make me feel like you don't like what we have been blessed with."

Naomi turned her back to Troy and took a sip from her water bottle so that he wouldn't see her rolling her eyes.

"I am happy, I just envisioned things a little different for us, a single home versus a row home, being in the suburbs versus the city, I don't know Troy just not right here in the heart of West Philly, right where we grew up, where everyone we know is still at, no change of scenery, nothing."

"Well it's good to know that you're ungrateful. I mean we're both only 26 years old, and this is our first home, we've only been married for two years, damn, give it some time."

Naomi snapped and cut him off.

"We don't have time, I never wanted to raise a child in the hood Troy."

She stormed out of the kitchen.

Troy walked after her grabbing her arm.

"Baby, you're pregnant, we're pregnant?" He asked.

She put her head down, and he lifted her chin as the tears rolled from her face.

"Yes, we're pregnant." She smiled and reached her arms around her husband.

"It's ok baby, just give me a year, I know the baby will be here before then, but we won't raise our child here, you hear me?"

He held her face to his and kissed her full lips.

"Just trust me Naomi, I love you and I'm gonna love that baby, trust me."

Troy was excited. He had the woman of his dreams and was about to be a father, he had to make good on his promise and get them out of the hood, he knew Naomi wanted better, and now with a child on the way so did he.

The next morning Troy was up and headed to work early, excited, and ready to request all the overtime he could in order to start saving for their new home. He looked over at his wife who was still sleeping, the sunlight peeking in on her clear chocolate skin. She was beautiful to him. Everything from her tall slender frame to her complexion and full lips. He had loved her since their high school days at West Catholic and now with her growing their child in her belly he was even more in love. He leaned over and kissed her gently on her forehead and was off to work.

In just a little while Naomi was awake. She had got a good night's sleep and felt optimistic about her family's future. Troy didn't make a lot of money but working in construction was a decent income. He was a hard worker and Naomi knew he did anything to keep her happy. She stood naked in her mirror looking from all angles at her belly. She couldn't believe that by the end of the year she would be a mother. Her belly was still completely flat and besides missing her period and having a positive test, there were no other signs of her pregnancy. She dreamed of how big she would get, if it would be a boy or girl and what they would name their first child. She smiled and finished getting dressed so that she could head to work.

Naomi hopped in her car and headed to work. It was a sunny May morning, and she admired all the beautiful single homes on her way to her job as a bank teller. Ever since she was transferred from the Center City location to the Havertown branch, she had fallen in love with suburban life. She daydreamed about she and Troy owning a single home, having a huge backyard, and raising their child in a decent school district. She prayed that all would work out and headed into work.

"Hey you." A squeaky little voice and bright smile greeted Naomi.

"Good Morning Eva. "

The two conversed in the break room while Eva fixed her morning coffee and prepared for the day.

Naomi was comfortable around Eva. She didn't have many friends, and she was an only child with no siblings so when she met Eva after her transfer, they instantly hit it off.

"I need a night out soon lady, we need to go hang out in Old City this weekend and have some drinks, I feel like an old woman lately."

The two laughed.

"I know, social life is on zero, maybe we can do dinner this weekend, I could use an outing." Naomi responded.

"Dinner, woman I want to let my hair down out of this bun, listen to some music and put on a cute lil' mini dress, I know you're married so your dress may be a lil' longer than mine, but the hubby shouldn't mind you going for a girl's night."

Eva looked at Naomi, partially concerned, hoping that her husband wasn't one of "those". The controlling, never want their women to go out type. She had only met him a few times, so she wasn't sure. Naomi picked up on the look she was giving her and responded quickly.

"Oh, hell no girl, Troy doesn't mind at all. Honestly, my husband is the sweetest, most understanding guy ever, no jealous or trust issues at all." Naomi genuinely smiled at the thought of how hard Troy worked for them and how he loved her whole heartedly. She knew he would be an awesome father.

"Ok so then yeah, dancing and drinking this weekend, woot woot!"

"I can't Eva, dinner and a movie is all I will be doing for girl's night for the next seven or so months." She smiled waiting for Eva to get what she was saying. Eva squealed and Naomi covered her mouth with her hand.

"Shhhh, no one here knows yet, I wasn't going to say anything until after I was out of my first trimester, but your ass keeps trying to turn me into an alcoholic, so I had to tell you."

"Oh my gosh, I am so happy for you girl, ok cool dinner and a movie it is, no alcohol for you, gotta keep everything in order for OUR little boo boo."

She looked around to make sure no one was looking and then bent over to talk to and rub Naomi's nonexistent belly.

"Get up crazy, before someone sees you." They chuckled and headed out on the floor to start work for the day.

The next three months were routine. Troy was working longer hours saving away getting ready for the baby and trying to move to a new neighborhood and Naomi worked and enjoyed seeing her belly grow. She was now almost five months pregnant and had a small baby bump. Her pregnancy was going smooth. She and Troy had just found out they were going to parents of a baby girl and were getting more excited each day. Troy's mother Diane, and Naomi's co-worker Eva each had been picking out names since they found out the gender, and The Jennings didn't like any of them.

Naomi sometimes got saddened that she had no real family to celebrate with about her bundle of joy. Her father had passed away when she was just eight, and her mother was killed in a car accident in her freshman year of high school. Her Aunt Margo was the closest thing to a mother she had but had moved to Virginia after Naomi and Troy were married to retire and live her life. Troy's mother Diane and Naomi often clashed, Diane was very opinionated, and Naomi felt like she sometimes overstepped her boundaries. Eva had become her go to girl. In just a short time, they had bonded, and Eva's Puerto Rican family treated Naomi like their own.

She got to work early so that she and Eva could have their usual morning girl talk. Everyone at work knew Naomi was pregnant by this time so Eva didn't have to hide her conversations and belly rubs with "Baby Jennings" as Naomi referred to her as.

"Good Morning baby love, how are you today, oh hey girl, how are ya?" Naomi rolled her eyes and laughed.

"Well hey to you too, I already see how this is going to go once I have the baby, just forget about lil' ole me huh?"

"Uhh something like that." She responded. They laughed as they counted their drawers to get ready for a busy Friday at the bank.

At almost noon, Naomi asked to leave the floor to go to the restroom. It had been nonstop since they opened at 9 am and the bathroom was calling her name. While in the restroom, she pulled out her phone to see a text from Troy that said he wanted to talk to her when she got in from work. She responded with a simple "ok we love you" and attached a picture of her standing in the mirror smiling in her mango-colored dress, with her little baby bump bulging. Troy was a natural talker, so she didn't think twice about what he wanted to talk about, it was probably something as simple as him trying to figure out what Sunday dinner would be. She shook her head at the thought and slid her phone back in her dress pocket and headed back out to work.

She opened the bathroom door to complete silence. Three masked men stood in different positions in the bank, guns drawn, holding all employees and customers at attention with their arms up. Naomi wanted to throw up, her first thought was to pull out her phone and call the police, but she decided against it. She then realized that none of the robbers had noticed that she had even opened the door, so as weak as she felt her plan was to just step back in the bathroom where she could quietly call the police and keep herself and her baby safe. She took a deep breath and one step back; she was sweating but knew she just needed to take two more steps back to be out of view and in safety. On her third step, she somehow lost balance, and the wedge heel shoe she was wearing tilted, she fell into the door, causing a banging noise causing one of the gunmen to turn to her. Her cover was blown, there was no escaping now.

"Get up and put your damn hands up and walk slowly out here."

Naomi was frozen she stood up but never began walking.

"I said put your fuckin' hands up, and walk slowly out here, let's go."

Still, she couldn't move. She thought of her husband and how she needed him at that very moment.

The gunman was anxious, he began walking towards her, shouting, but she couldn't hear him. He then raised his gun and continued walking in her direction.

Eva screamed and ran towards the direction that Naomi was standing. In no time, another gunman began firing towards Eva, causing chaos. The gunshots ignited adrenaline in Naomi, as she saw her friend being shot at. She began to run, only to fall at the exact time that Eva did, she was in pain but looked up slowly holding her hands up off the ground, because she was being demanded to do so by a man, who stood over her with a gun to her head, and a heavy boot in her back pressing her growing belly into the ground. She couldn't speak, scream, or cry, she peeked up to see Eva lying face down in a puddle of blood. Naomi blacked out.

Chapter 2

"I'm fine, I don't need to be sitting in here all day feeling sorry for myself like I'm handicapped, besides we need the money your unemployment and my sick leave pay is not cutting it, we're falling behind and before we know it, we will be in an even worse area, back in an apartment." Naomi snapped.

"Listen, I don't know what part of you're not going back to work yet you don't understand, I never demand anything of you Naomi, but today that stops, I am your husband and you will not be going back to work tomorrow, and that's it. Not only did you see your friend get killed less than a month ago but the whole ordeal caused you to lose our daughter."

Troy was hurt. He walked over to Naomi who was standing at the closet looking for something to wear to work the next day.

"You don't think you need some time to heal, not physically but emotionally, because I wasn't the one carrying the baby or who saw my friend murdered and I'm still fucked up about it, so I don't know how you think you're ok." He stood behind her and wrapped his arms around his wife, out of habit he slid his hands down to her belly as he would normally have done. She pushed him back.

"STOP IT TROY, I'm fine and I am going to work tomorrow, we need money. We have to get the hell out of this neighborhood as planned."

"Fuck the plans, I'm your husband and I said you're not going back yet and that's final. We'll manage financially."

"Manage? That's the problem, you're ok with just managing, I'm not. I'm a grown woman and I'll be at work tomorrow so that I can MANAGE to get the fuck up outta this neighborhood with or without you."

She slammed the closet door and stormed out of the bedroom.

Troy couldn't believe it. She had become cold over the past couple of weeks, she wanted no comforting, no compassion, nothing from him. He felt unwanted, but knew he loved his wife. He knew that she wasn't ready to go back to work, but Naomi was stubborn and relentless in her pursuit of a better life. He had to play his part and find a new job. The same day of the bank robbery he had been laid off. He knew what Naomi said was true though, unemployment and her being out would cause them to start slipping, and he had to be able to buy them a new house as promised. Naomi was serious about getting out of West Philly, and Troy wanted to make his wife happy. He got dressed and left out to go meet with the only other woman he had ever loved, his mom.

"I don't know mom, it's like she is hell bent on moving and I get that, but I just don't feel like she should be going back to work so fast after what just happened."

Troy leaned his head back in the leather recliner in his mom's apartment. Diane walked over towards him with her satin robe on, holding a small plate with some fresh baked corn bread on it.

"Here baby. I made this when you said you were stopping by. She sure isn't, she's not thinking straight, and I don't know what's gotten into her lately with this whole, get out of West Philly shit she's talkin' bout', as if the home you provided for her isn't good enough. There are so called men out here that ain't worth a dime, don't work, can't stay out of jail, and you have worked since a teen, and did everything right by her, asked for her hand in marriage, bought her a car, a house, and it's still not good enough for her, just ungrateful if you ask me." Diane shook her head and lit a cigarette. Troy didn't like his mother talking about his wife, but he did agree with her.

"Right, but I mean I understand where she's coming from, especially when we were expecting the baby, wanting for more, better neighborhood and schools, but I just know we have to take care of ourselves first, and now with me being out of work, that year plan to get a new house isn't so realistic. But she says she's out with or without me."

"With or without you, well shit let her go, any woman who lost a baby a month ago and talking about moving some damn where with or without her husband is up to no good." Diane was disgusted.

"Come on now ma, Naomi isn't up to anything, I do agree she comes across a little ungrateful right now, but she ain't up to anything." Troy was confident in his words even in his mother's side eyes and mumbles. He and Naomi had problems, but trust was never one of them. He talked with his mom for a little while longer, before he headed home to try one more time to convince Naomi to stay home, and if it didn't work, he would support her decision as hard as it was to do so.

Chapter 3

Naomi sat in her Honda Accord for almost ten minutes before heading into the bank. She clicked her alarm, took a deep breath, and confidently walked through the front door. It was completely silent, exactly how it was on that day when she came out of the bathroom. She placed her hand on what used to be her growing belly and felt hot, Eva's face flashed before her. She wasn't ready, tears welled up in her eyes and she started to make a dash for the door, and suddenly her supervisor Alexandria appeared.

"Welcome back Naomi, you look great." She extended her arms and gave her a warm hug.

"We have some goodies in the break room for you, donuts, fresh fruit, bagels, come on back we are all excited and want to make sure you feel ok being here."

Naomi smiled, but she knew she wasn't up to it, but couldn't return home. She went on for hours with Troy about how she knew she was ready, and she wasn't about to hear him say "I told you so". She sucked up her tears and was able to get through her day, and every other day for the next few weeks.

Although Naomi was back at work, money was still tight. Troy was still looking but was getting frustrated because he had now been out of work almost three months and unemployment only lasted six months. The pressure was on. He sent resume after resume, did application after application and still no job. He was getting hard on himself but not harder than his wife was.

He decided to clean the entire house and make dinner by the time Naomi got home. By 5 pm the house was spotless and smelled delicious. Troy had prepared his famous stuffed salmon. Troy hopped in the shower once dinner was done, besides trying to make Naomi happy by cooking and cleaning, he also hoped that his gestures could possibly lead to some romance from his wife. He understood right after she lost the baby and had never pressured her, however her doctor had cleared her a couple of weeks prior and since then, they hadn't so much as kissed. Troy was confident it would be the night. He missed and needed his wife. As Troy headed down the stairs fresh out of the shower with his basketball shorts and wife beater t-shirt on, Naomi was headed in the front door. He hurried down the stairs and kissed her on her lips.

"Hey baby, how was work today, I missed you." He asked.

She kicked off her heels, and responded, "It was fine."

Troy knew Naomi had her days since she had been back at work, because he knew in her heart, she wasn't ready to return, but he supported her decision and went with the flow. Today was no different, he continued to try and love on his wife.

"Well hopefully just fine can turn into a good day, I made dinner, the house is cleaned, so you can eat, shower and cuddle with your husband for the rest of the night How's that sound?"

"It sounds like you're getting too comfortable with being a stay-at-home husband, did you get any calls for an interview today?"

Naomi's words pierced through Troy's ego. He was upset and felt disrespected.

"What the fuck are you talking about, because I tried to help out my wife by preparing a meal and cleaning the house that we both live in, I'm comfortable being a stay at home husband? That's crazy Naomi. I think you forget I've worked since high school, this is the first time I have been without a job, and it's only been three months, and although it isn't my full income, I do still provide for us and pay bills."

Troy was livid, he swung open the refrigerator door, grabbed a beer and popped the top.

"I never said you didn't Troy, however how comfortable can you be here, our house is small as hell, the neighborhood sucks, I mean you honestly feel comfortable with weed smoke filtering in our bedroom window at night or hearing gunshots? This is depressing to me and I just don't understand why it's taking you so long to find a job. This whole situation stresses me out."

Troy couldn't believe his wife, she was definitely ungrateful, but he loved her with everything in him. He stared at her for a minute admiring her beauty. Her big brown eyes were filled with tears and Troy knew he had to put his foot down.

"More than the neighborhood we live in, the size of our house, the gunshots, none of that matters, the real issue is that you're an emotional wreck, you have no business being back at work right now after losing our child and seeing your friend killed, you can fool your coworkers, but not me. You need to go into work tomorrow and let them know you need more time off. No ifs ands or butts about it, now let's sit and eat before dinner gets cold."

He pulled out a chair at their table and waited for his wife to sit.

"I'm not hungry, I'm headed up to get myself ready for work tomorrow." She never looked at Troy, simply turned away and headed towards the stairs.

Troy was frustrated. He slammed his bottle of beer on the counter and went outside on the front porch for some fresh air.

Chapter 4

The Jennings household was tense for the next couple of months. Troy was still out of work and only had one more month left to receive unemployment. Naomi was still working at the bank, just to not be in the house with Troy, and they had only had sex one time in five months. They barely talked and Troy often fell asleep on the couch, whenever he did sleep. Diane noticed that her son was changing. She came by one afternoon while Naomi was at work to visit.

"When you going to the barbershop, I ain't never seen your head looking like that. You know you have hair like your father's side so you need to moisturize and brush it at least, damn."

"Ma, I ain't thinking about no damn haircut, I need a job." He replied.

"Yeah but if they call you about a job, you can't show up looking like this. I wish you would go see Dr. Riley, you need to talk to someone."

"Ma please, lay off me a lil' bit, I got this, I made an appointment, it's for tomorrow, I just don't know how I feel about going to see a shrink, I feel fine."

"That's what you say, but you aren't eating right, not sleeping, and stressing trying to keep up to some standards that ungrateful wife of yours has set, I'm worried about you."

Just as Diane was talking Naomi walked in and slammed the door.

"You should be mindful of speaking about someone in their own home, especially when windows are open and you're sitting there calling me ungrateful."

"Oh, so today you're calling it your home, feels good to come home and have a place to lay your pretty little head doesn't it?"

Troy stood up.

"That's enough, I'm not going to have my wife and my mom going back and forth with one another, enough is enough."

Diane stood up and she and Naomi stood making intense eye contact for a few moments before she walked towards the door.

"Troy, take care of YOU, and call me if you need me."

Diane never looked back and walked out of the door.

Naomi headed towards the kitchen to pour a glass of wine and began talking to Troy.

"So, is that what happens every day while I'm at work?"

Troy looked at her confused and walks right past her.

"You and your mother sit here and have conversations about how ungrateful I am."

"Listen, leave it alone Omi, it's over with."

"It's not over with, I walk up to our home and all I hear is your mom talking about how ungrateful I am, and you didn't even try and defend me."

"Defend you for what, you are ungrateful, ever since the day we moved in this house you've done nothing but complain, and I've put up with it, even agreed to get us out of here."

"Which doesn't seem like it's going to happen anytime soon." Naomi snapped.

"And guess what when it's supposed to happen is when it will happen, not a day before, I'm killing myself inside trying to make you happy, life happens, let me get through this rough patch, and I'll do whatever you want because I love you, but don't keep kicking me while I'm down."

Troy looked his wife in the eyes and began to cry. Naomi felt no compassion.

"I'm trying Troy, but do you know how hard it is working in a bank around money all day, helping customers and having access to see their accounts and then I look into ours and get depressed."

"Who are you? When did you become such a money hungry bitch?"

Troy knew he was wrong. He was immediately apologetic, but not before the red wine that Naomi had poured was splashed all over his face. She stormed out of the kitchen and Troy stood emotionless trying to understand what happened to his life.

He sat up all night as usual, surfing the internet for positions. He prayed for his marriage and finding employment. He stood up in the living room mirror and knew he needed to talk to someone. His mother was right, and he couldn't talk to her because she was already against his wife. He also couldn't talk to Naomi if it wasn't about having found a job or a new house and none of his friends even knew he was going through what he was.

It was almost five in the morning before he fell asleep on the couch and when he heard Naomi up getting ready for work he jumped up. Although he had only an hour and a half of sleep, the last thing he wanted was of for her to come down ready for work, and he still be asleep. As a part of his routine over the past five months, he headed in the kitchen to make coffee for his wife, which most days she didn't drink. She came downstairs with her long black hair pulled back into a ponytail, wearing a pair of aqua blue trousers, and printed top. She was beautiful to Troy. All he wanted to do was make her happy and make love to her every night. They exchanged good mornings and just like that Naomi was out of the door, Troy home alone.

He stood in the mirror again and knew he had to get himself together. Troy was slightly over 6ft tall and was never a slim man, his weight looked good on him though. However, with his eating habits and lack of sleep, he had lost weight, and it didn't look good on him. His full face was slim and looked droopy. He hadn't smiled in months and that was his best feature. His hair was all over his head, and he needed to get it cut, but his car insurance was due, and he had just paid his cell phone bill and his portion of the mortgage, and he wasn't about to ask

Naomi or his mom for money for a haircut. He decided he would go to the appointment with Dr. Riley. He hopped in the shower, washed his hair and made it look as good as it could considering he needed a haircut.

Troy was frustrated as soon as he got to center city. He missed being at work, making money and keeping busy, he prayed that he would receive a call back soon. He was only eligible to receive two more checks from unemployment.

He walked into the small office on 12th and Chestnut and signed his name in. The receptionist was pleasant and quite attractive. She stood up to grab paperwork that Troy needed to sign and he couldn't help but get aroused by her figure. The lack of affection and intimacy in his marriage was becoming a problem. He hurried to sit down before it became noticeable and filled out all the paperwork. Once in Dr. Riley's office he felt a little uncomfortable. He wasn't sure what he would be asked, what to say or if any of it would help him at all.

Dr. Riley was a pleasant older black doctor. He didn't wear a suit and tie, didn't use big fancy words, Troy could relate to him. He felt comfortable speaking about his issues about work and in his marriage. The forty-five-minute session flew by, and Dr. Riley had some recommendations for him.

"It was a pleasure talking to you today Mr. Jennings. You definitely have some things going on that can cause the issues I see present. I definitely feel that you are suffering from depression and insomnia. A lot of people are against medications for such conditions, however in your situation, I feel that in order for you to be able to be productive and find employment you will need to first be able to rest, which is what the Zolpidem is for, and to be able to be positive and remain focused you will need the Lexapro."

Troy sat up.

"I don't know about all that medication doc, I mean I ain't crazy at all."

"No, Mr. Jennings, that is the common misconception in the black community, it has nothing to do with you being "crazy" it is about stabilizing issues and being able to control them so you can function properly. But I understand, it is a lot to take in, I have written the prescriptions, on the way out on the first floor stop by the pharmacy and have it filled, think about it, talk to your wife about it, and then take them if you decide to. But please make an appointment with Portia out front to see me in two weeks."

Troy stood up at the same time as Dr. Riley and shook his hand.

"Will do Doc thanks again."

He had no problem making an appointment for two weeks or thinking about the medication, but he was in no way talking to Naomi about it, she wasn't even going to know he went. He waited for a few minutes for the prescription to be filled and headed to his car. He threw the two bottles in his glove compartment and was ready to roll. Troy had decided to surprise his wife at work. He used his last ten dollars on flowers and headed over to the bank.

Troy was excited to see his wife. She loved flowers and it had been a long time since he had surprised her. He walked in and saw her beautiful smile, it made him smile. He hadn't seen it much as of lately. He started to walk over to give her the flowers then realized she was with a customer. He admired her from across the bank, just waiting to present his queen with flowers. Troy's smile turned into a slight frown as the male customer lifted Naomi's hand and kissed it before he walked away, causing Troy to see red. He took off walking fast towards the man.

"Ayo that's my wife."

Naomi noticed his voice and immediately came from behind the counter.

"Troy what the hell are you doing here?" She mumbled under her breath.

"I was coming to surprise you with flowers, but I see someone else has your fuckin' attention." He shoved the flowers into her chest area and walked towards the door following behind the man. He noticed that he had dropped a slip of paper and picked it up before exiting the doors behind him. Naomi wanted to follow him, but he had caused enough of a scene, she quickly walked to the trash can, dumped the flowers and went back behind the counter as if nothing happened.

By the time Troy made it to the parking lot, the mystery man had hopped into his vehicle and slid his sunglasses on his face. Troy didn't know what kind of car it was, but it was something foreign, something that cost a lot of money and something he could not afford. He yelled for him to stay away from his wife, as he sped off, almost laughing. Troy felt defeated, he hopped in his car and looked at the deposit slip of Mr. David Randall. He slammed his hands on his steering wheel in anger, he was a millionaire, and he was probably the reason Naomi was no longer interested in him anymore.

Chapter 5

Troy was upset and needed someone to talk to, but he knew that if he went to his mother's house she would go on and on about her dislike for Naomi, and that she would make it her business to confront her. He just wanted someone to vent to, and wanted the responsibility of working out his marital issues on his own. He decided to stop past his longtime friend Naeem's apartment. They had been friends since their days at Hamilton Elementary and he knew Naeem would listen and give honest advice if needed.

Naeem was the ultimate bachelor, had never been in serious relationship, but was always honest to women about his intentions. They knew he wasn't looking to be in a committed relationship, but his good looks, sense of humor and gentleman like qualities kept him busy with dates. Women respected his honesty, although many of them thought they would be "the one" to change his mind, it hadn't worked yet.

"Nigga, what's up with your cut, what you growing dreads or something?"

Naeem always had a joke, but Troy wasn't in the mood for it, and didn't want to have to let his homie know that he didn't have a haircut because he didn't have the money.

"Man fuck all that, I'm tryin' to deal with some real shit."

Troy was serious, he felt like his marriage was falling apart.

"So basically, you saying you feel like the Mrs. Is cheating on you with someone that come in to her job?"

"Basically. It just all adds up, her rushing to get back to work so soon after losing our baby and seeing her coworker killed, how she's been worrying about moving into a better neighborhood complaining about money and shit all the time, and today was just the final straw, I'm showing up to her job to surprise her with flowers and she's smiling and shit in some guy's face."

"Damn, that's crazy, so what did she say. Who is the dude?"

"I only know his name because on his way out of the bank he dropped his deposit slip, he had just deposited some money in his account."

He passed the rectangular piece of paper to Naeem.

"God Damn, what the fuck he do for a living, this shit says he just deposited $30,000, and do you see his available balance. I hate to say it homie, but seeing this, and hearing what you said about how she's been about money and shit lately, it really does all add up. She's intrigued by this nigga's money, I wouldn't be surprised if he's been sliding her a few dollars on the low, has she come home with any out of the ordinary purchases, you know like expensive shit?"

Troy was already pissed, but Naeem had added fuel to the fire that was already festering in his mind. His biggest fears were in front of him, he knew if he didn't get it together his wife would be leaving him sooner or later. His mind was frantic, he sat at Naeem's for another hour, barely listening to him talk. His mind was racing, from thoughts about losing Naomi, finding a better job, and even wanting more information on Mr. Randall, he needed him to leave his wife alone.

When he arrived at home Naomi was in the shower. He opened the bathroom door wildly, startling Naomi.

"You're just popping up everywhere today I see, you know what you did today was not only."

Troy cut her off.

"Listen save the lecture you think you're about to give me like I'm your fuckin' child about earlier, just be upfront and honest with me about your behavior, what's going on with you and Mr. Randall, is he the reason you're taking a shower right after work, you normally don't until later in the evening after dinner, so what's up Naomi JENNINGS, you do remember you're married right?"

He was serious, she turned the shower water off, and snatched back the shower curtain to stare directly in Troy's eyes.

"What are you talking about, my behavior? I was at WORK, doing my JOB, have you become that unfamiliar with the idea?"

Troy was enraged, he lunged towards Naomi and raised his hand as if to smack her. He caught himself and snatched at the shower curtain causing the rod to fall down.

"You have lost your mind."

Naomi grabbed her towel off the hook on the door, wrapped it tightly around her, and stormed past Troy.

"So that's what you're going to do, ignore me, I don't deserve to know what's going on?" He yelled.

Naomi stopped in the hallway and turned around to face him.

"You know what you do deserve to know what's going on, and what's going in is I am going to go and pack a few things and go stay at my cousin's house until you calm down and realize that your behavior is not acceptable, I am your wife, but you don't own me."

"Oh, now you're my wife, were you my wife when you were flirting with another man at work today? I'm sorry I can't deposit $30K in our account like he can, he's the reason you've become so worried about bigger houses and neighborhoods lately, right? So now that I've confronted you about it how conveniently you decide to go stay at your cousin's house, right. Let me tell you this, if you walk out of OUR home with clothes and stay out overnight, don't you dare come the fuck back."

Naomi stood in the hallway, still undressed, with tears flowing from her face. She knew Troy was stressed but he had never talked to her in that manner, she was scared and had no other option but to leave. She headed into their bedroom, put on some yoga pants and a tank top, threw some items in an overnight bag and headed down the hall towards the stairs. Troy sat on the couch, still visibly angry. They glanced at each other and Naomi looked away quickly. She walked past the couch and turned the door knob. Troy's voice startled her.

"Remember what I said, you stay out tonight, you're confirming my thoughts and you can stay where you are Naomi."

He never looked up at her. She took a deep breath and opened the door, closing it gently behind her. By the time she reached the bottom step outside, she heard something being tossed in the house. She knew she had made the best decision.

Troy was a wreck. He sat up for hours contemplating everything about his marriage. He knew Naomi was seeing someone, even if it wasn't David Randall. She was cold, disrespectful and heartless to him. They weren't making love, they barely hugged or kissed. There was no one he wanted to talk to other than Naomi. He ignored calls from his mother and Naeem all night. He called Naomi back to back for a half hour straight, to no answer. He even called her cousin Shayla, who she said she was going to stay with, no answer as well.

"I'm her husband, it's after midnight and she isn't answering." He repeatedly mumbled to himself as he paced back and forth in the living room. Before he knew it, it was almost 2 a.m. He was tired but couldn't ease his mind long enough to rest. He decided to give those medications from Dr. Riley a try. He needed some sleep, because the first thing in the a.m. he would be talking with his wife to figure this situation out once and for all. He headed to his car to grab the medication. He hadn't eaten all day so he went to the kitchen and made him a peanut butter and jelly sandwich and grabbed a glass of orange juice, to prevent upsetting his stomach. He headed upstairs and took a quick hot shower to try and relax. He slid into their bed, tossing and turning in agony smelling the scent of his wife's fragrance, imagining her being in the arms of another man. Before long the medicine had begun to work, and Troy was relaxed and getting much needed rest. He knew he needed to fix his marriage or let it go forever.

Chapter 6

Troy awakened to the bright summer sunshine across his face. He stretched his arms out while lying in their king-sized bed hoping to feel his wife next to him. She wasn't there. He couldn't believe that Naomi had actually stayed out. The feeling of being refreshed from a good night's sleep instantly left, and anger and frustration filled his heart and mind. He picked up his phone and called Naomi, no answer even after three back to back calls. It was after 9 a.m. so she had to be at work, and couldn't answer. He felt a little comfort in knowing that but still needed to see her and talk to her. He decided not to go to her job, because that would only make the situation worse, so he would wait until after she was off from work.

The time was moving slow, Troy wasn't able to do anything except think about the different scenarios that could play out once he talked to his wife. He needed honesty. He needed to know was she cheating on him, what he could do to make her happy and again and most importantly if she still loved him. He briefly thought about the upcoming hardships they would face if he didn't find a job fast. There was only a month left until his unemployment would run out. He needed a job fast, but the first order of business was to get things right with his wife.

He stood in the bathroom mirror staring blankly at himself. Despite getting a good night's rest, he still looked tired, his honey colored complexion wasn't glowing like it normally would, and the dark circles under his eyes told his story. His hair was still all over his head, and his thoughts were racing. He leaned down into the sink and splashed cool water on his face in hopes to not only cleanse his face but to wake up from the thoughts in his mind. It was almost 4p.m. and Naomi would be leaving work shortly.

At 4:11 pm Troy called his wife's phone, there was no answer. He waited a few minutes more, assuming that she had gotten caught up at work. By 5:26pm after 17 calls, Troy still had not heard from Naomi. He was clueless as to why she wouldn't even answer his calls. He hopped in his car and headed to her job, it was Thursday, one of the bank's late nights so maybe she had stayed. He just needed to see her car and know that she was ok. He pulled out of his parking space only to realize that he wouldn't be going anywhere. His car was on E, and he had no money for gas. Troy quickly turned the corner and headed back to his house. Once he parked he punched the steering wheel in anger.

Naomi had no real friends that Troy could call and question, he knew she had to be with David. He began to rummage through her belongings, pocketbooks, pants anything trying to find out information on David Randall. He had ruined their room, there were clothes everywhere, and Troy was in a rage. He headed downstairs to log onto his computer, he sat down and began typing in the name of the man he believed his wife was with. He found no specifics, and any detailed information needed to be paid for, and he had no money.

He sat motionless on the couch, looking at the flashing light on the answering machine. He jumped up hoping it was Naomi. It wasn't her, but it was someone calling about an interview for a job he had applied to. The interview was in two days and he now had no choice but to talk to his mother about everything, because he needed money for a haircut and gas for his car.

Diane had no issue stating her disdain for Naomi as Troy sat trying to eat oxtails and rice she had prepared.

"See this is what I hate, one of your favorite meals and you can't even eat all behind an ungrateful, worthless woman who is obviously out here laid up with someone else"

Troy interrupted.

"Mom please, I'm frustrated enough, you've been going on about Naomi since I've been here. I know you're upset, but so am I and she's my wife. I came here to simply ask to borrow the money to get a haircut and some gas to get to this interview, that's it, I really don't have it in me to even think about Naomi at this moment."

Troy got up from the table and grabbed his almost full plate of food.

"I'm sorry baby, and I understand, I just don't like seeing you like this."

She reached for Troy's plate and begun to store it in a plastic bowl.

"Take this home, if you get hungry later, you'll have something to eat."

She reached out and hugged her son. They held each other tightly, both fighting back tears. When they let go, she reached into her bra and pulled out three one hundred-dollar bills.

"Mom, no I don't need this much, I just need to put gas in my car and get a haircut that's it, all I need is about fifty dollars and I'll give it back to you next week."

"Fill your tank up, go get your haircut and be ready for those jobs to keep calling you for interviews. And I don't want the money back, I just want you to be ok, I love you Troy."

"I love you too mom and I appreciate you, but let me get out of here. I know it's going to be a long night; Naomi and I have a lot to talk about."

Diane held her tongue and wished her son a safe walk home. Luckily, she lived close enough to walk to her house considering his gas tank was on empty.

Troy turned the doorknob of their cozy home on Felton Street. He called out for Naomi but she didn't respond. He walked slowly through the house, tidying up some of the mess he had made while in a rage. Since Naomi hadn't arrived home, he thought the least he could do was have the house cleaned so they could talk and get back on the right track. After he was done cleaning, he finally had an appetite and decided to heat up the oxtails from earlier. The oxtails were delicious, but it was almost 10 pm and his wife still was not home.

He called her phone several more times, the first few it rang, but by the fifth call, it was going straight to voicemail. Troy tossed his phone on the bed and decided to take his medication to get a good night's sleep. He had a plan for the next day that involved him going to the bank to demand that his wife have a conversation with him. He knew they had issues, but he wasn't giving up on the love of his life. He showered after he took his medication and drifted off to sleep staring at a picture of Naomi holding her tiny baby bump just months prior.

Chapter 7

It had been over a year since Naomi's disappearance. She never returned to work at the bank, no trace of her even after filing a missing person's report. The months of searching for her combined with Troy being named as a person of interest initially had taken a toll on him. He thought over and over about the hours he spent at the police station being questioned and damn near bullied by detectives assuming he had something to do with her disappearance. He was eventually cleared but not before he became depressed about no longer having his wife and being looked at as the perpetrator.

Besides no traces of Naomi, the account belonging to David Randal, had been wiped clean and closed just three days after Naomi's disappearance. Troy knew in his heart that's who she was with. Her phone, although it was still on, hadn't rung in months, but Troy still called it at least once a week, and continued to email her a few times a month, hoping she would respond. He was devastated.

After losing his home six months after Naomi's disappearance, he had moved into his mother's tiny one-bedroom apartment. He slept on her couch and had the same routine day after day. Up at 4 am and heading to work at a warehouse, to right back to his mother's apartment to eat dinner, shower, and get ready for the next day. He had no social life or any desire to do anything else. Countless times Naeem had invited him out for drinks, parties and any other guy's night and Troy always declined. Naeem always invited him knowing he would say no, but was shocked when he finally agreed to go to a Sixers' game.

Diane was excited to see him getting dressed and heading out to have some fun. She stood watching him from her bedroom door like he was a teenager, while he brushed his hair and beard. Troy was looking better. Although he was still stressed and upset about Naomi's disappearance and losing his house, having a steady income and eating his mother's home cooked meals daily, had helped him gain some weight back. He had treated himself to a Polo Sweat suit and a fresh pair of Jordan's for the game. He was looking forward to the Sixers vs Lakers game so that he and Naeem could talk shit all night. He was a die-hard Lakers fan and Troy felt the same about the Sixers.

"I just don't understand how a nigga could be so hype about a team from another city, shit is crazy man, look at you with that nut ass yellow jersey on." Troy laughed.

"You ain't gotta understand shit about me or this jersey, worry about your bum ass hometown heroes." Naeem shrugged his shoulders as Troy laughed and shook his head.

They headed to their seats to enjoy the game. After a few beers and plenty of trash talk, the Lakers were victorious.

"Nigga you talked all that shit about my jersey, now look at ya ass, quiet as a church mouse." Naeem laughed loudly.

"Man, please It was a good game, and we still play two more times this season, we whipped ya'll asses the first time we played so we even."

"Whatever nigga, we gone see though next month. I mean ya'll not a championship caliber team so it really don't even matter, ya'll may not make the playoffs." He laughed while Troy was shaking his head. "But uh' what's up with the shorty whose number you got at the game, you thought I ain't see you nigga." He reached out to shake Troy's hand.

Troy reluctantly shook his hand and tried to change the topic.

"Listen I get it, and I'm not trying to press the issue, you've had a rough couple of years, which is why more than anything, you deserve to have a little fun and to be happy." Naeem who was normally a jokester, was serious and sincere.

Troy leaned back in the comfy seats of Naeem's Denali and exhaled deeply.

"Yeah Man, shit just still don't seem real. It's like my life went from bad to a fuckin' nightmare. Me and Naomi start having issues, then we lose our child, she disappears, I lose everything and now here I am, sleeping on my mom's couch. I just don't understand."

"I hear you man, but don't punish yourself or deny yourself a good time any further. All bullshit aside, you a good dude Troy, you deserve happiness."

Troy sat quiet for a moment thinking about everything that had transpired and Naeem was right, he deserved to enjoy life.

"Thanks man, appreciate it. But uh yeah, that's Taylor, Taylor Hayes. You don't remember Taylor from out Overbrook Park? You probably remember her older sister, Morgan, she went to Overbrook, might have graduated a year before you."

"Oh yeah, they used to call her "Make it Rain Morgan." The two started laughing.

"She was in like 11th grade and a stripper she was fast. Had niggas in their late 20's up at the let out. She ain't talk to nobody her age. I ain't gonna lie, you know I was never the type to be scared of a girl, I would shoot my shot at anybody, but as bad as Morgan was, I was shook, I wouldn't even look at her in her face, no bullshit."

"Yo, you a wild bull, but I feel you, she did have that type energy with her. But Taylor was always quiet, with glasses, didn't hang out, none of that. She went to Goretti, so you probably ain't see her much. She was always a cute girl growing up, but she looks good now, a whole grown ass woman."

Naeem agreed.

"Yeah man, you gotta hit her up. But on some real shit, I ain't intimidated no more, what's up with big sis, where Morgan at?"

"Man, I heard she fuck with some NFL player or some shit out LA." Troy replied

"Damn, still outta my league." They both laugh.

"But for real nigga, live a little, hit Taylor up, at least go out for some drinks, get you some yams, something nigga."

Troy laughed and shook his hand as he hopped out of the truck.

"Alright Bro, I'll holla at you, be safe."

Troy heads in and peeps in his mom's room to notice that she was asleep with her glasses and her light and tv on. He shook his head and smiled as he removed her glasses and kissed her on the cheek. He turned off the tv and the light as he headed out to the living room. He plopped down on the couch and slid his sweat suit off and laid down. His first thought was Naomi and how much his life had changed so fast. He shook his head and laid with his eyes open wide for a few moments and couldn't stop thinking of Taylor.

He picked up his phone and thought to call her but didn't want to appear too anxious, so he texted her.

It was good seeing you earlier, hope you made it home safe.

He sat his phone down, not expecting to hear back from her, at least not right away. His text notification startled him. It was Taylor. They continued to text well into the night, and even made plans to go out.

Chapter 8

Troy was excited to finally be moving into his own place. It had been a year since he had been staying at his mom's place. It was a rainy April day as Troy loaded up his belongings from his storage unit and headed to his apartment in Ardmore.

"That's everything, I just need to stop past mom's crib and grab my clothes. Man, it's been a crazy couple of years, a lot of shit happened that I never would have imagined, I still can't wrap my brain around Naomi disappearing and ..."

Naeem was sympathetic about everything his friend had been through, but wasn't a fan of the disappearing act by Naomi. He cut him off mid -sentence.

"Yeah man I get it, and I know you been through a lot, and you had no control of any of it unfortunately. Not the bank robbery, not the lay off at work and for sure not your wife running off to be with a millionaire."

Troy interjected.

"I don't know if that's what happened, I still feel that something happened to my wife man."

Troy was getting upset and Naeem felt himself getting annoyed.

"I get it man, but at the end of the day, we don't know what happened and you can't keep living in that misery. Man, you've been down for a while and things are finally looking up for you. That promotion at work, your own place again, things are going good with Taylor, I'm just saying, don't let the past fuck up your future." He reaches out to shake Troy's hand.

"I feel you, 'Preciate you. I still can't believe your client was willing to rent me the apartment for that amount, I can't wait to get in there and hook my shit up."

"That's what I'm talking about, my nigga is back!" The guys shook hands and shared a brotherly hug before they hopped in the UHAUL truck and headed to pick up the rest of Troy's things.

It was almost 7:00 pm by the time Troy had moved everything in. With the help of his mother and Naeem, he was able to set everything up and unpack. He was eager to be comfortable in his own place and wouldn't sit until no box was left unpacked.

"It looks good a cozy in here son, I like it." Diane smiled

"Thanks Mom, is cozy code word for small?" They all laughed.

"No not small, comfortable and warm, it feels like a home, you haven't had that in good while, I'm happy for you."

She reached out and pulled Troy in for a tight hug.

"Now, Naeem what time you heading out, I'm ready to get back to my place and relax, you mind dropping me off?"

"No problem Ms. Diane, I'm ready when you are."

As they began to prepare to leave there was a ring at the door bell. All three of them look around at each other wondering who it could possibly be.

Troy heads to the door and opens it and instantly smiles. It was Taylor, straight from her shift at Lankenau hospital where she was a nurse. She stood in the doorway of the apartment in her navy-blue scrubs, smiling with her long highlighted blonde hair pulled back in a ponytail. She had some grocery bags in her hands and held them up for Troy to grab.

"Hey love, I stopped and picked you up a few things on my way here."

Troy grabbed the bags and leaned in to give her a kiss.

"Tay, you've been working hard all day dealing with patients, you really didn't have to."

"Man please, work is always gonna be work, I wanted to be sure to bring you some food, paper plates and cups because you know you hate dishes, oh and a few of those fig and coconut scented candles you like."

Troy smiled as she walked past him and up the stairs that headed to his second-floor apartment. Taylor was short and petite, with a beautiful smile and high energy spirit. Her aura comforted Troy. He smiled as he slowly walked up the stairs hearing Taylor's high-pitched voice excited to see his mother and closest friend. They were equally excited, although he often thought of Naomi and still loved her, he knew Taylor was an excellent partner for him.

"That was so sweet of you Taylor to pick these things up for Troy, he's not used to this kind of thoughtfulness from a woman." Diane stated.

As much as Troy knew what his mother said was true, he hated that even in Naomi's absence, she still felt the need to throw shots not considering his feelings at all. He restrained from saying anything, but encouraged Naeem to head out and take his mother with him. They all said their goodbyes and before long, Troy and Taylor were alone enjoying a bottle of wine.

"Listen I did not know that Giant's rotisserie chicken was that good Tay."

"It's called working smarter not harder boo, so many nights after a shift at work I'm dead ass tired and hungry, but don't want crappy fast food, that chicken is a life saver. Grab that, and a bag salad, and just like that a decent meal with no prep time, woot woot." They burst into laughter.

"You always woot woot'in lady, with your fine ass." Troy kissed her passionately as they sat on the couch.

"Mmm seems like you ready to bless your new place." She kissed him again and gently caressed his face with her hand and slowly ran her hand down his chest to massage his manhood.

Taylor stood up and gently pulled Troy up from the couch. She led him into the bedroom walking him slowly and seductively down the hallway. Troy admired her from behind, her toned petite body, her long blonde highlighted hair and her overall softness and femininity.

Once in the bedroom, Taylor dropped to her knees, undressed him from the waist down and orally pleased him while he pulled her hair gently with his eyes closed.

He pulled her up and kissed her wildly. She climbed onto his bed on all fours, looked back at him and laid her head down. Troy paused momentarily and ran to the bathroom to grab a condom and headed back into the bedroom. The candle light and silhouette of Taylor's body excited him as he entered her love slowly.

He gripped her waist and followed her lead as she slowly rocked back and forth from the base to the tip of his manhood. Troy could feel that she was making it about him, she turned to her back and opened her legs wide and waited to feel the warmth from his body. She gasped as he penetrated deeply into her and droplets of his sweat dripped onto her full breasts. She gripped and caressed his back and before long he let out a sexy moan indicating his satisfaction. Taylor trembled gently and smiled as she too had climaxed.

Troy kissed her gently and laid beside her caressing her breasts and feeling happier than he had in a long time before they both fell fast asleep.

Chapter 9

Troy smiled at his phone, Taylor had texted him and asked if he was in the mood for tacos, it was Tuesday and she made a mean chicken taco and delicious margarita. He had enjoyed his day off running errands, getting his haircut and even stopped by to see his mom. Although he was looking forward to tacos later with Taylor, his mother had left over lasagna for lunch and he was still stuffed.

Troy pulled up at home and was excited that he had enough time to shower and relax before Taylor arrived. He walked in and threw his keys on the counter and grabbed a bottle of water from the fridge. He headed to his bedroom and got undressed. The steam from the shower felt great as jazz music played softly throughout the apartment.

Once out of the shower, he laid back on his bed daydreaming about everything that had happened over the previous two years. He was happy that his life was changing for the better, but he couldn't help but wonder how life would be if Naomi hadn't lost their baby or disappeared without a trace.

He sat up and dug through his nightstand and pulled out a business card. He grabbed his phone and decided to call Detective Bryant Ross. He was assigned Naomi's missing person's case when she disappeared. Initially he would reach out to Troy to update him, although it was always the same update, that there were no leads regarding her.

"Detective Ross speaking."

Troy took a deep breath and responded.

"Hey how you doing Detective, this is Troy Jennings, husband of Naomi Jennings."

Troy stood up and walked to the living room and paced while he awaited his response.

"Yes, hello Mr. Jennings, how are you?" He responded.

"I'm doing pretty good, just wanted to reach out because I hadn't heard anything about my wife's case and just wanted to know what happens if she isn't located, is the case closed, do we still search, I'm just confused and need some clarity and closure."

"I understand Mr. Jennings, I know this must be difficult for you. In being completely honest, cases like your wife, become extremely difficult as time goes on. If I'm not mistaken it has been over two years since her disappearance, there were no signs of foul play, no sightings, nothing. In my opinion and through my years of experience, it appears it was well planned. There's no flight records, no phone records, no records of her living anywhere else. This may be difficult to hear Mr. Jennings, but if your wife is still living, she doesn't want to be found."

Troy swallowed hard, and wiped the tears that were rolling down his face. His voice trembled as he thanked Detective Ross for his time.

"You're welcome, I'm sorry Mr. Jennings, hang in there."

Troy laid down on the couch emotionless and tossed and turned for quite some time before he decided to take his medication. When Dr. Riley first prescribed it, Troy used it every night to sleep and focus, but once he began working again and some sense of normalcy was restored in his life, he only took it if he absolutely needed it. He still saw Dr. Riley once a month and he felt that his visits were beneficial to him. He walked into the bathroom and grabbed the two pill bottles. He took both. He walked out of the bathroom and headed to the living room to grab his phone that he left on the coffee table.

When he walked into the living room, he stood there shaking his head. He looked over at the vase by the television, the same vase that Naomi loved and had to have before they moved into their home, he then looked at the couch, the same couch he slept on for months waiting to hear his wife walk through the door. He snapped. He picked up the vase and tossed it into the television, then headed over and tossed the couch, he ripped his paintings off the wall and then headed to the bedroom. He opened his closet and tossed everything on the floor trying to get to the gray box. He kept a box of her belongings in his closet as not only a keep sake, but a hope that she would one day return. He opened the box and began to pull apart the clothing items inside. He was in a rage.

Troy was breathing hard and began to tire, he sobbed as he sat on the side of his bed. He was heartbroken. It had finally hit him that wherever Naomi was, she wanted to be there. He knew he had to get on with his life, and this episode was the proof. He laid down and drifted off to sleep.

A couple of hours later, Taylor arrived at his apartment. She had called to tell him she was on the way but he didn't answer. She thought nothing of it, they had already agreed that she would come over and cook, she figured he probably was watching something sports related not paying his phone any attention. She called again, when she pulled up because she needed help, she not only had the groceries but her overnight bag for work in the morning. When he didn't answer she decided to get out of the car and ring the bell. There was still no answer. She knocked on the door and called his phone simultaneously, hoping he would hear one or the other. She was beginning to be nervous.

A door opened and startled Taylor. It was the neighbor, he said he had heard some yelling and bumping around a few hours earlier but nothing since then. She thanked him and decided to call the police and Ms. Diane.

"I can't believe you called the police and my fuckin' mom because I didn't answer the door." Troy was upset.

"I can't believe you're upset with me for being concerned with your well-being." Taylor was in disbelief, not only at Troy's reaction, but at his apartment. It was in complete disarray and chaos. He was irate and all over the place. She had never seen him like this.

"Troy that's not fair." Diane interjected.

"Mom please, this has nothing to do with you."

Diane snapped.

"Like hell it doesn't, I am YOUR mother, I watched you hurt and lose it all behind a woman that walked out on you, just disappeared into thin air without a god damn care of what it would do to you. I've seen you build yourself back up and meet someone who genuinely cares about you, and you're treating her this way because she gave a damn? That Naomi really did a number on you boy, she got you feeling like someone giving a fuck is a bad thing."

Taylor looked at Troy confused, she picked up her purse and headed towards the door. Troy yelled out for her to wait, but she never looked back. He looked at his mother and shook his head before heading to his bedroom and slamming his door.

Chapter 10

It had been three weeks since Troy had seen Taylor. Although they had been in contact through text or talking on the phone, Taylor had refused to meet with Troy. When they began dating, Troy had never disclosed what happened between he and Naomi and simply stated that they had divorced. She felt betrayed and in hearing Ms. Diane talk about their marriage she was demanding to know the full truth. Initially, Troy was hesitant and felt no need to explain or relive his marriage to Taylor. However, he was beginning to realize that he had true feelings for Taylor and wanted to be as honest and forthcoming as possible, especially because Naomi could not do that for him.

It was a beautiful Saturday in October. Taylor had agreed to meet Troy at his apartment after her hair appointment and lunch with her sister and friend. Her beautiful curls blew in the wind as she walked out of the salon and placed her oversized Christian Dior sunglasses on her face. Taylor was beautiful, educated and had a great personality, she knew she could have any man she wanted but it was something about Troy.

Taylor was the first to arrive at The Love restaurant in Center City. She headed in to be seated and pulled out her phone to text Morgan and Ivory. Ivory was looking for parking and Morgan said she was five minutes away, Taylor knew for sure that she hadn't even gotten in the car yet. She shook her head and begun to look over the menu.

Before long, Ivory walked up to the table in typical Ivory fashion, thigh high hot pink boots, fitted jeans and the fluffiest hot pink ostrich fur off shoulder blouse. Her face was beat, and her hair was in a neat ponytail. Ivory was ironically, beautifully brown in complexion. Her father was Italian and her mother just knew she was going to be fair skinned and named her Ivory. She would jokingly tell people her name was Honey, just to hear them say, that the name was fitting.

"Hey Tay Tay." Ivory stood at the table with arms wide open waiting to hug her dear friend.

"Honey Girl look at you, looking beautiful." Taylor replied as the two embraced.

Ivory did a little twirl for Taylor for her to get the whole effect.

"The hair is flowing mama, Nikki curled the shit out of it."

"Why thank you, yes you know I don't let anyone touch my shit but Nik." Taylor replied.

The pair sat down and ordered two strawberry mimosas and started chatting to catch up with each other while they waited for Morgan.

"So, wait, I'm so confused. Yall have been together for about a year, everything is pretty much perfect, and then you find out he's still married, the wife disappeared and he's still in love with her? This shit sounds out of a movie."

"It sounds like pure bull if you ask me." A soft voice replied.

"That's why I ain't ask ya ass." Taylor playfully rolls her eyes and stood up to hug her sister Morgan.

Morgan stood awaiting the love from her sister and friend looking flawless. The black bodycon midi dress fit her hour glass figure like a glove, and the addition of the orange blazer and Balenciaga track sneakers, gave her the perfect balance of sexy and sporty.

"Hey sister hey friend, what did I miss?" She asked as she sat down at the table.

"Two rounds of mimosas and Tay catching me up on the deets about her and Troy." Ivory answered.

"Well let me just order us a whole bottle of champagne, that will cover me catching up to yall, and my advice with the whole Troy situation remains the same, get rid of him and get you a baller. That's it! Now let's move forward with planning our annual Girls Getaway, 2020 will be here before we know it." Morgan picked up the menu and proceeded to signal the waitress to place her drink order.

"See that's why we don't like telling your ass shit." Ivory laughed.

"No for real, everyone ain't as cold hearted as you Morg." Taylor was annoyed but played as if she wasn't.

"I'm not cold hearted, I just don't believe in wasting my time. Like I said when you and I talked Tay, I do like Troy, he's a decent guy, I mean I feel like you could absolutely do better financially, and by the way, did you call Micah's teammate? Girl, he has an even better contract than Micah and like two endorsement deals, you better hop on that." Morgan tilted her head and sipped from her glass of water.

"And he's also only 21 years old, I don't have time to raise no man."

"But you have time to deal with someone who clearly isn't emotionally ready to move on? Please give me the young bull with the dollars any day over a man working 9-5 AND still hung up on an ex, okay." Morgan and Ivory high five.

"For the record Tay, I'm neutral, I'm not for or against Troy, just hearing everything out, I just ain't wanna leave Morg hanging." They all laughed.

"But seriously, I love him and I want it to work. Ya'll know me, I'm not concerned with how much a person makes, MORGAN." She looks at her sister who rolls her eyes.

"Of course, I'm not about to be with no bum ass nigga, but Troy works hard, he has dreams and a plan to reach them, he doesn't need me to handle his responsibilities, and he treats me like a queen. I do have some reservations over the ex-wife or whatever the hell she is, since the incident, and we are supposed to meet later today to talk and for him to explain everything that he hadn't before, and I'm open to hearing him out." She sipped her drink.

"You know what sis, that's fair. I know I'm always on you about the type of guys I keep trying to force on you, that's just me being an overprotective big sister, wanting you to have all you deserve and more, but I get it and I respect you for being who you are and being willing to talk through issues and feelings with someone you care about, because a bitch like me, moving on to the next one as soon as I feel a way." They all laugh.

"And I truly need to work on that, little sis, you are inspiring me to work on me." Morgan smiles and sends air kisses across the table at her sister.

"So, it's safe to say, you'll get to the bottom of what's going on with Troy and make a decision based on what he divulges?" Ivory asks.

"Exactly." Taylor responded.

"Ok perfect, sounds like a plan, let's get into these shrimp and grits and the plans for our getaway, I have a date later on and I need to get some beauty rest before I head out." Ivory does a cute dance in her seat.

"Oullll, ok girlfriend, make sure you call us tomorrow with all the details. One thing my girl gonna do is date and have a good time." Morgan smiled.

"You know this." Ivory replied.

They sat for another hour enjoying their food, planning for a trip to the Dominican Republic in the spring, and sipping on delicious cocktails. At almost 3 o'clock, they said their goodbyes and headed out of the restaurant. Taylor called Troy to assure that he was home and still up for talking. She was nervous, because although she knew that she wanted what her and Troy had to continue to grow and last, she had no idea his true feelings regarding her or Naomi. She pulled out of her parking spot, took a deep breath and headed to Troy's apartment.

Chapter 11

"So basically, your wife began wanting a better life, you obliged but lost your job, the bank she worked at was robbed and she lost a child, you suspected her of cheating, ya'll get into a bad argument, she leaves and you haven't seen her since then?" Taylor asked.

"In a nut shell, yes." Troy responded.

Taylor sat on the dark gray sectional, with her hand on her forehead, quiet for almost two minutes. She was trying to digest all that she had heard about Troy and his marriage before she spoke, it was a lot to take in.

"Talk to me Tay, what's going on in your mind?" Troy look at her intently wanting to hear her response.

"I'm trying to process it all Troy, when we ran into each other at the game and started talking, when you spoke about your marriage, you didn't mention any of this. You said ya'll grew apart and divorced, and that's not the truth." Taylor was upset, but calm.

"I get that Tay, but do you know how hard it is to keep replaying the story and having to explain it, I just wanted to keep it simple so that we could get to know each other as adults." He stated.

"But that isn't how that works Troy, even if I say ok I understand you not detailing every aspect when we first started talking, it's going on two years that we've been together, you've had time and opportunity to tell me the whole truth. I mean after what happened here a few weeks ago, my main concern was were you emotionally over Naomi, now the main concern is the fact that you aren't even divorced, ya'll are still married." Taylor shook her head and stood up.

Troy stands up and gently grabbed her hand.

"Tay come on don't walk off, we haven't seen each other in almost a month, let's figure this out." He pleaded.

"I just don't know, seeing you like that the other week, how emotionally attached you still are, the baby, her disappearing and you believing her to just be with another man is a lot. So, what happens if she pops up out of the blue one day and you have all these unresolved feelings, what happens to us, what about me or my feelings? Did you consider that when you were keeping everything from me? I just don't know where I fit into all of this. I want to be married and have children one day, we can't be married Troy, legally you're still married to her." Taylor began to cry.

"Tay, I know it is a lot, but do you believe me when I tell you that I love you." He lifted her chin and looked her in the eyes.

Taylor was shocked, although they had been together for almost two years, neither of them had told one another that they loved each other. She had confided in her sister and Ivory, but never to him because he had never said to her.

"I love you too Troy. I'm scared though." She said softly.

He kissed her full lips gently and asked her why and explained that through everything he had been through with Naomi, he had never felt loved. He explained that her thoughtfulness and pure heart won him over from the start and that he didn't want to lose her.

"I don't want to lose you either, but I don't want to end up hurt because of whatever is unresolved between you and Naomi." She stated.

"You won't, I promise you. I know I had a moment a few weeks ago, I'm not gonna lie, that shit gets heavy mentally, but I haven't seen or heard from her in almost four years and a lot has happened, but I can stand here confidently and say that I love you and want to build a life with you. Whatever Naomi and I had is over. I'm human so yes at times I wonder not even about us as a couple but just is she ok, did she really just want to be with someone else, is she even living, I think that's normal, she literally disappeared into thin air. But, if she were to pop up today or tomorrow, she couldn't come between what you and I have, I'm in love with who you are and how you make me feel." He hugged Taylor tightly.

Taylor held on to Troy tightly and rubbed her hands up and down his back as she quietly sobbed with her head in his chest. She trusted him and wanted to be with him and build a life together. She also was no fool. She knew there were loose ends that Troy needed to follow up on in order for them to move forward and she made it clear to him.

Troy was in agreeance. He didn't want to lose Taylor and was willing to do whatever to make sure she knew he was serious. Not only was counseling important, she also made it clear that he needed to get the information and start the process of divorce from a missing person. They vowed to work to build their relationship and be together forever. They ended their night making love and holding each other in their arms until they fell asleep.

Chapter 12

Troy pulled up at home from work exhausted. There were a bunch of workers out sick over for a few weeks and he had been taking as much overtime as he could. He and Taylor were in the process of purchasing a fixer-upper and he wanted to be sure to be prepared financially. Their plan was to move into the property for a couple years after the renovation, and then to use it as a source of income as a rental property to purchase their dream home.

He walked in the apartment door and immediately took his work boots off. Something smelled delicious, but he couldn't quite figure out what was cooking, but he was ready to enjoy it. Taylor's shifts at the hospital were long and draining, so cooking daily, didn't quite fit into her schedule. But, at least once a week, on a day off, she threw down in the kitchen. She often made more than one meal so that there were leftovers throughout the week to eat. This day was no different.

"Hey Tay, it smells like heaven in here, what you making?" Troy asked as he walked up behind her and smacked her firm butt and kissed her neck.

"Come on now." She playfully whines as she turned around to give him a kiss.

Troy rubs his hands together looking at all of the delicious food that she had prepared. Honey glazed salmon, macaroni and cheese, cabbage, and a pot of chicken and shrimp alfredo. He thanked her for cooking and complimented her on how well everything looked and smelled before proceeding to smack her booty once again.

"You love it when I smack that ass, stop that."

Taylor smiled and rolled her eyes as they both laugh and she thanked him and asks him how his day at work was.

"Busy as hell, I had three guys out today sick, it's a little virus going around." He responded, and grabbed a piece of chicken out of the pot.

"Troy stay out of that damn pot." She yelled and shook her head.

"I told you weeks ago the Coronavirus would be starting to be an issue. We've had so many positive cases in the past few weeks, it's honestly scary. I've been a nurse for almost seven years and I've never seen anything like it."

"I just don't get it, it's essentially a cold right, I mean a real bad cold, so I don't know why it's becoming such a big deal."

"Because it affects so many functions and body parts. Just think about having a bad cold, the flu, an upper respiratory infection and diarrhea and stomach issues all at once, not only would you feel horrible, but your organs would be working twice as hard to do their jobs." She explained.

He understood more after that explanation and they went on to enjoy their dinner talking about everything from the Coronavirus to Troy being interested in starting his own contracting company and Taylor wanting to step back into being an artist.

"Don't get me wrong, I love my career, it's great, I have no complaints whatsoever, but my artwork makes me happy, keeps my mind free and not to mention it can be a decent second source of income for me. I don't know, it's just been on my mind lately." Taylor twirled her pasta with her fork thinking about it all.

"You just gotta do it baby, on your days off, take some time for you and your art. Once you get some pieces down have an art show, put yourself out there."

Taylor smiled about his excitement to her interests and making sure she was completely happy. Those were the qualities she admired the most and what also made her the most nervous. Taylor's mind wandered as Troy talked about her and her artwork and him taking more contracting side jobs in hopes of starting his own company in the near future. She worried about Naomi often. Although, Troy had assured her that he was committed, knowing how good of a man he was and how he supported her, she couldn't understand why Naomi could just up and leave and always felt that she would return and ruin what she and Troy were building.

"Hello Taylor Renee Hayes, report back to earth." Troy waved his hands trying to get her attention.

"You ok Tay, what's on your mind?" He asked.

"I'm sorry babe, just like that I got an idea in my head for a painting, I zoned out a little bit, what were you saying?" She lied. They vowed to not bring up Naomi and she didn't want him to know that she even thought of her.

"Ahhhh see, the creative juices flowing already. And yeah, I was asking if you thought Solid Brick Contracting was a good name for when I step on out and launch the business? I'm not ready as of yet, still have a bunch of smaller side jobs coming up and making sure the team is solid, but for the most part I think I can count on Naeem for sure, Javier, his brother and my man Everett to build with."

"Troy, I love that name, I'm so excited for us, so many plans to put into play, but we've got this. TEAM US!" They hi-fived and lifted their wine glasses to toast. Troy smiled and repeated "TEAM US", as they sipped their wine and enjoyed the rest of their dinner excited about what the future held.

Chapter 13

Taylor stood in the break room at Lankenau hospital rushing to finish her lunch. The hospital had been bombarded with Coronavirus cases and the staff couldn't keep up. The hours were long and it was quite scary to everyone, not knowing the severity of it all.

As soon as she took her last bite of her rice bowl her cell phone rang. It was Ms. Diane, and she immediately panicked. She never called her phone, they would always text to keep in contact and share inspirational quotes to one another, but never a phone call. She answered quickly.

"Hey Ms. Diane, is everything ok?" She asked.

"No, the job just called me, Troy has been hurt at work and they are rushing him to the hospital. Lawd, I pray he is ok." Diane responded frantically.

"WHAT? Ok what hospital?"

Taylor was worried but tried to remain calm for his mother. She could not leave the hospital during her shift as they were already short staffed due to the virus that was spreading rapidly, but someone had to be there for Troy. She decided to get Ms. Diane an Uber to Roxborough Memorial hospital and she would join her there as soon as her shift was over in a few hours.

She was sidetracked the remainder of her shift, texting with Ms. Diane, eagerly awaiting updates. 3:30 pm took forever to arrive, and Taylor clocked out on the dot and headed to her man. When she arrived, she was told that she wasn't able to enter his room as he already had a visitor and they were limiting them due to the Coronavirus. She understood, as her own workplace had begun to implement the same policies during what seemed to be a health emergency. She texted Ms. Diane to let her know she was there and hoped for un update.

Before long, Diane walked into the waiting room and Taylor stood up, they hugged and from the hug Taylor knew he would be just fine.

"Thank you for coming Taylor, I appreciate how much you love and care for Troy."

She squeezed Taylor's hand.

She proceeded to explain that he had slipped off of a ladder at work trying to replace a lightbulb in the main warehouse. His arm was broken, he had a concussion and they suspected a torn ACL in his leg, but they still needed to confirm with an MRI. Overall, Troy would be good, Taylor was elated to hear that nothing was life threatening.

He was released from the hospital the next day in pain but in good spirits. His mother would be at his apartment during the day while Taylor was at work to help him out. It was confirmed that his ACL was torn and he would be having surgery to repair it in a few weeks, in the meantime, besides the cast on the arm, he needed a cane to get around due to the pain from his knee.

"Here ya go, I made you some cheese eggs, grits and some bacon, I'll grab you some orange juice in a minute. How you feeling?" His mother asked.

"Thank you, mom, and I'm ok, still can't believe I fell like that, and still have to get surgery on my leg, this is slowing me up on some things I'm trying to get done. I feel like my whole life, every time I make progress or plans to move forward with something, I get a setback. Just like when I was ready to start saving before and got laid off and Naomi ended up..." Diane cut him off.

"Alright now, life happens, just like you bounced back before, you will this time around. Just focus on getting yourself together and everything will fall into place as it should."

Diane was getting out of the habit of bad-mouthing Naomi, she also didn't want him bringing her up. She loved he and Taylor together and didn't want the person who walked out on her son to interfere in their growth as a couple.

The doorbell rang and Diane looked at Troy wondering who it could be.

"Oh, yeah that's probably Naeem mom, he said he would stop by today." Troy said.

"Ok well eat your grits before they get cold, I'll let him in and bring you the orange juice." Diane headed to the door and greeted Naeem before heading in the kitchen for the juice.

"Yo bull." Naeem yelled as he walked into the bedroom.

"What's up Na, they got a nigga laid up." The pair laughed and shook hands.

"You'll be back right in no time."

"Well shit after I get this cast off my arm, I have to have surgery on the ACL and be down another six weeks or so, this shit crazy." He thanked his mom who had brought the orange juice in the bedroom.

"You're welcome, ya'll need anything, I'm about to go in this living room and watch my programs."

"I'm good Ms. Diane thank you." Naeem answered.

Naeem and Troy continued their conversation.

"Yeah but man it ain't shit to even do right now this the best time to e down. Everything is shut down due to this virus."

"Man, this shit is wild, how long has your job been closed? And according to Tay, it's gonna be awhile, she said the cases at the hospital have skyrocketed, she working overtime like shit, moms been pretty much staying here because by the time she gets in from work, and get a shower, she is rocked, a couple nights she ain't even eat dinner that she cooks before she goes to work" Troy said.

"I believe you, my job been closed for two weeks now. But I ain't complaining, I'm making more money from home than I was going in every day." Naeem laughed.

"What you mean?" Troy asked.

"Nigga that Pandemic unemployment is love. You just file a claim online and they send you a debit card and they paying the regular rate plus an additional few hundred a week. I'm stacking that shit, and I'm about to apply for the PPP loan, for small businesses." Naeem clapped his hands and shook his head as if his plan was top tier.

"Nigga what business? And that unemployment sounds like love, but I'm already getting my worker's compensation money from work."

"Any business you put on the application, they not checking that shit. You can get your worker's comp and the unemployment. You remember Tone from down North, you used to work with him a few years ago? I ran into him last week at the market, he filed an application a couple weeks ago, said he had a barber shop, got $15k. Didn't you get the LLC for your contracting business? You better use that shit nigga, get this free money while you can. Once you on your feet again, shit will be easier for you to get Solid Brick off the ground with some extra coins." Naeem was serious.

"Yeah it sounds good, man. It sounds real good. All I think about is getting the business rolling and being able to buy a house, invest in some other shit and buy this woman a ring and chill." Troy was serious.

"And man, you know I ain't even the settle down type bull, but I'm with you on this one, Tay really the one for you bro. That shit sounds like a plan, if you need me to help you with the applications and shit let me know, the lil' shorty Kira I deal with, do them jawns, she charges $350, you get the money in like a week."

Troy was happy to hear what his good friend thought of his relationship with Taylor. It confirmed that he was on the right track. He took Naeem up on his offer and applied for both the unemployment and PPP loan. He was ready to start putting everything in motion for their future, this plan was full proof.

Chapter 14

It was a mild October morning and Troy and Taylor enjoyed a light jog on Kelly Drive. Troy felt great, to finally be active again after his ACL surgery three months prior. They both had committed to incorporating exercise and eating better into their daily routine. They both felt great.

Taylor had been working nonstop since the start of the pandemic, but she promised that when she was off from work to take care of herself. She would spend her mornings exercising and her afternoons painting. Troy's job was still closed and he was receiving unemployment while getting his feet wet with his contracting business.

Between all the hours Taylor was working and the additional funds Troy had due to unemployment and the $35,000 he received for the PPP loan, they had money for the down payment of a home and to invest in Taylor's artwork and Troy's contracting business. While his job was still closed, he took on small jobs for friends and family and started to get referrals beyond that. He had just finished the basement renovation of one of Taylor's co workers which led to another hiring him.

"Babe you really did a great job at Olivia's home, she's been showing those pictures all week." Taylor laughed.

"That's what's up, I'm glad she liked it. I'm just happy to be doing what I love again. I know this pandemic shit is crazy and unpredictable, but it's been a blessing in disguise to me, shit everything has, the injury at work, covid, it's all helped me start a new chapter. I have no complaints." He lifted his water bottle up and took a big sip.

"Well speak for yourself, because I am tired and it doesn't appear to be an end in sight." Taylor rolls her eyes and pulled her hair back and wrapped a ponytail holder around it.

"I know it's hard for you right now baby, but all your hard work will pay off, not just at work. Your art show is coming up, it's going to be dope and let's not forget closing day for our home." He smiled.

They were two weeks away from closing on their home. They had settled on a four-bedroom two-bathroom home in Drexel Hill. It was spacious and had all the features that were their must haves from an on-suite bathroom to a garage and updated modern kitchen.

The art show was beautiful. Taylor was stunning in a two-piece orange pant suit. The pants were high waist and accentuated her curves. She wore a plain white blouse and had the perfect gold accessories to compliment the orange. She wore her hair and a curly ponytail and opted for a natural looking make up look. Troy was dapper in a pair of brown dress pants with a cream-colored fitted sweater. He stood back sipping cognac while admiring Taylor. Art was her passion and she was in her element.

A friend who owned an event space had allowed Taylor to use the venue, as most were still closed due to Covid-19. There was a maximum of 25 guests allowed and masks were mandatory. She had the idea to also livestream the art show and allow viewers to purchase online. The pandemic had changed a lot of things and she didn't want to have to push her debut back any further, she was ready so she adjusted and did what she needed to do.

Morgan and Ivory arrived and greeted Troy. They all stood watching Taylor describe a painting that she titled "Eternity". There were beautiful shades of purple and gold on the painting and she described how it symbolized her everlasting love for the arts and being true to your authentic self. The crowd of about 20 people were attentive and captivated by her work. Diane and her good friend Joanne stood front and center admiring the work of Taylor. As Morgan winked at Troy he noticed Naeem and his date Kira arrive and he knew it was time to start the show.

He walked over to Taylor and gently grabbed her hand. She looked nervous and unsure of what was going on but she still smiled at him and turned to look at the guests. Troy got down on one knee and Taylor covered her mouth with her hands as she realized what was taking place.

"Taylor Renee Hayes, you have been a blessing over these past three years. You have loved me unconditionally while staying true to yourself and pursuing your own dreams passionately. I admire everything about you. Your beauty is the icing on the cake, who you are is pure and authentic and that is what I love the most about you. I want you for eternity, will you marry me?"

The emotions ran heavy in the room as Taylor accepted the proposal and proudly extended her left hand to receive the two-carat princess cut solitaire from her future husband. The newly engaged couple kissed and hugged while their loved ones and guests and enjoyed a champagne toast with remarks from Diane, Naeem and Morgan. As if the night couldn't be any more perfect, Taylor sold 7 paintings and made over $5000. T.R. Hayes was making a name for herself in the world of art.

She was in awe the entire ride home, holding out her hand and staring at her beautiful ring.

"Tonight, was absolutely amazing, I can not believe I am going to be Mrs. Taylor Renee Jennings. Babe, I love you, I was so not expecting this. We talked about getting our house and decorating it how we wanted it and the business and my art, getting all of that off the ground first. I mean I knew we would get married, especially after you took those steps to become officially divorced, but this shocked me, big time." She was overjoyed.

"I know we talked about all of this before, and with us closing on the house next week, me getting things moving with Solid Brick and your debut, what better timing. I'm just happy you like your ring, that's a big decision." Troy laughed.

"I absolutely love my ring, you did great hubby." She leaned over and kissed Troy as they pulled into the Wawa parking lot.

"Babe get the apples with caramel please I need something sweet, other than me." She laughed.

"You so corny Tay." He smiled and shut the door of his truck.

As he walked into the Wawa, he felt his phone vibrating in his pants pocket, he pulled it out assuming it was Taylor with another snack request. His heart started beating fast and he began to sweat as he looked and saw the name NAOMI on his phone screen. It only rang three times and then stopped. He looked around as if someone could see her name or even knew who it was calling. He walked to the back of the store and pressed her name, the phone rang, versus all the other times he had called and it went straight to voicemail.

The voicemail was full. He thought to send a text but decided not to. He had just proposed to the woman he was in love with, he couldn't allow Naomi to interfere in any way possible. He put his phone back into his pocket, grabbed the snacks and headed home.

Troy and Taylor made love to celebrate their engagement and the success of her art show, but he was distracted and hoped that Taylor hadn't noticed. Well after Taylor had drifted off to sleep, Troy paced the living room contemplating his life. He knew Taylor was the perfect woman for him, but he longed to know what went wrong with him and Naomi and where she had disappeared to. He called the number again with no answer. It was late and he was exhausted but could not rest. He took some of his medication, drank some water and decided to email Naomi. He sent the email and put his phone on the nightstand. He kissed Taylor on her forehead and drifted off to sleep.

Chapter 15

Troy was awakened by the smell of his fiancé's body wash flowing into the bedroom from the bathroom. He stretched and immediately reached for his phone to see if Naomi had either called, texted or emailed him. Other than a text from his mother, there was nothing. He thought to try and call, but Taylor had just turned the water off and was getting out of the shower. He sat his phone down and walked towards the bathroom.

"Good morning baby girl?" He grabbed her wet face and leaned in to kiss her.

"I know you lying dragon breath, you better let that brush hit that tongue." She laughed and turned her face to the side to receive a kiss on the cheek.

"Nah never mind now." He smacked her naked wet butt instead.

"Babe." She playfully whined.

"You know the rules, no kisses cool, take this ass smack." He popped her rear end again and leaned in and tried to kiss her.

She pushed him away, he grabbed for her and she took off running.

"You remember I was a track star in high school right." She laughed and jumped on the bed, he reached out his long arms and grabbed her arm. He climbed on the bed and smacked her backside again. This time she turned and smiled sexily at him and dropped down to her knees and began to caress his manhood and pulled his underwear down with her teeth. She slowly inserted it into her mouth and looked up at him while she pleased him. Not long after she began, Troy gently pulled her hair enough for her to release her mouth from his love. He ran his finger through her wet hair and motioned for her to turn over. She obliged and laid her head on the bed and awaited his entrance. Troy gripped her waist and slowly stroked her gently. Taylor gripped the sheets and breathed heavily as she began to move at a fast pace. Troy moaned and grabbed her hair. Before long, he had released himself inside of her and gently kissed her on her back.

Taylor rolled over and threw a pillow at him.

"How you end up getting' some and ain't even brush ya damn teeth, I can't stand you."

"You know you love me." He rolled over and kissed her lips.

"Ahhh got ya." He yelled.

"Troyyyyyy oh my god." She wiped her lips, rolled her eyes at him playfully.

"Can you believe I'm going to be Mrs. Jennings." She held her hand up admiring her ring.

"Of course, I can believe it, I asked you, can you believe it?" Troy laughed.

"I actually can't. If I'm being honest, I didn't think this would ever happen."

"Why? You didn't think I loved you?" Troy asked in a serious tone.

"No, I knew you loved me. I just wasn't sure the love you had for me could overpower your love for her." Taylor looked directly at Troy and her words made him nervous and uncomfortable. He quickly stood up and wrapped his arms around Taylor. He assured her that she was all he needed and he couldn't wait for her to be his wife.

In his heart he knew Taylor was the one, but his mind wondered about Naomi often. He initially always assumed she was dead, as there were no traces of her anywhere and he was in denial about her being with someone else. But the call from her phone number now had his thoughts racing. He knew he had to move on though, but needed to know how.

Taylor dreadfully got ready for a shift at the hospital. She had always loved being a nurse but, between the virus running rampant, the success of her art show and the excitement of their engagement, she wasn't looking forward to a long 12- hour shift. She would have much rather to stay at home with Troy and talk about the upcoming closing on their home, make wedding plans or paint. But, she was committed to her career, so she prayed, kissed her fiancé and headed to work.

Troy was meeting up with Naeem at his house to talk about a new job he had secured doing a basement renovation. They both were still not working due to Covid and receiving unemployment benefits. They had also each received a significant amount of money from a

PPP loan and decided to become partners with Solid Brick Contracting. The remainder of the money from the loan was given to Taylor for the purchase of their home. It bothered him at times that he wasn't able to take care of Naomi the way she desired, so he vowed to never be in the situation again. Taylor deserved it all, and he was prepared to provide it.

"I can't believe the amount of work we've been getting in the middle of a pandemic." Troy said.

"Man listen, everybody got money right now and nowhere to go, so they may as well make their cribs comfortable." Naeem laughed.

"No bullshit, I can't wait until next week for settlement, we don't have much to do, but I'm definitely putting my touch on that basement. I ain't gonna lie, I was a little apprehensive when we first started talking about buying a home, not because she ain't the one, but the mortgage only in her name, because I lost the other house." Troy shook his head.

"Nigga please, with a woman like Taylor, that shit don't matter. Once ya'll get married add your name to the deed and you're good. You should have been worried when you and that first wife of yours got the house together." Naeem laughed as he went to pour he and Troy another drink.

Troy knew that between his mother and Naeem, they always found a way to bash Naomi, and although she deserved it, because part of him believed she was still alive, he didn't want to hear it. He mentioned that he had a missed call from her number and instantly regretted it.

"What? A missed call? You called her back? Man, I would have blocked her fuckin' number so fast yo. You sure it was her? I'm sure they gave that number to someone else by now."

"It's still on because I pay the bill." Troy shook his head.

"Our phones were in my name, and initially when she disappeared it was on the hopes of hearing from her, but after I realized that wasn't happening, I just continued to pay it out of habit."

"So, let me get this straight; your wife leaves you without warning to be with another nigga, you meet a real one, finally get the divorce, propose to the real one, but you still paying the phone bill on the last one?" Naeem asked.

Troy just shook his head.

"On some real shit, you have to let that shit go dawg. Even if she is out there alive and well and that's her calling you, so the fuck what. I get it, you may still have a thought to want to know if she's living or not because I ain't gone lie, it's a wild situation, but at the end of the day it's been like four years and you living life right now. Thorough ass wifey, the business, about to have the home you dreamed about, the shit Naomi wasn't willing to wait for, so don't let her ass fuck up what you been working hard for."

Naeem lifted his glass of cognac and took a sip.

"I know, shit is crazy, that whole situation. But what's crazier is, I think it's so easy for me to think about Naomi and wonder because Taylor seems too good to be true. Shit just seems unreal that you can really be locked in with someone and no dumb shit be going on. We really a team and that makes me nervous like it's a dream or some shit, you get what I'm saying bro?" Troy looked over at Naeem and awaited his response.

"I feel you and you know I ain't even into all that relationship shit, but Taylor is the real deal, don't fuck that up. Block that fuckin' number, better yet, get that shit disconnected."

Naeem was serious and Troy could feel it. He knew he had something special with Taylor and he had to completely cut ties with the thought of Naomi. He blocked the number and planned to have the phone disconnected. He and Naeem went over ideas for the upcoming project before he headed home to his fiancé.

Chapter 16

It was finally Spring, Taylor's favorite time of year. She loved being on their back patio with her easel, paint and her wine glass in hand letting the warm breeze inspire her. She loved everything about their home and couldn't wait to be married and have children.

Taylor had taken much needed vacation time from work. The demand of work had been stressful, but there was finally relief in sight as the virus had began to slow down some. There was no vacation planned, just time off to concentrate on her art, their home and plans for their Summer of 2022 wedding. They had a little over a year to get everything together and it was starting to make her nervous. They hadn't decided on anything yet.

She was surprising Troy with his favorite, oxtails and rice. Ms. Diane had given her the recipe and they had been cooking for hours, she wanted them to be just right for her future husband. She carefully lifted one out of the pot and sat it on a plate to cool before she bit into the tender, deliciously seasoned meat. She picked up her phone and thanked Ms. Diane for the recipe, and in return, she thanked her for being such a good woman to her son.

Taylor gathered all of her items from the patio and put them away in the mudroom where she stored it all. She headed upstairs to get showered before Troy got home. Just as she pulled her beautiful blonde highlighted stresses back into a ponytail, she heard the front door open. She slid into her flip-flops and headed downstairs.

She walked into the kitchen and stood there with her hands on her hips, until Troy noticed and almost dropped the lid to the pot.

"Troyyyy why would you put ya damn hand in the pot? Ain't even wash your hands." She shook her head.

"Well damn baby how was your day?" He said sarcastically.

"Don't even try it, you know you dead wrong." She laughed and shook her head.

"My day was great, I started a new painting and I was able to get the recipe from your mom, as you can see." She rolled her eyes.

"And they taste wonderful. Oh and, can I see the painting?" He asked.

"Not quite yet you know I like to perfect it before I show you my work. How was your day?" She got on her tippy toes and gave him a soft wet kiss.

"Mmm it was ok, but it's going better now."

Troy pulled her close and slid his hands down to palm her butt cheeks. Taylor pulled back and told him to get showered so they could eat.

"That sounds like a plan. I need that for dessert though." He smiled brightly.

"We'll see." Taylor laughed pulled out a bottle of wine and two glasses. She couldn't wait to sit and have dinner to talk about their wedding and starting a family.

"Babe you got the recipe down pat. I ain't gone lie, your oxtails might be over mom's oxtails." He scooped his last forkful into his mouth and took a sip of the sweet red wine.

They sat at their kitchen table for hours talking about their wedding and decided on a destination wedding in Jamaica. It would be the perfect reflection of their personalities.

"Now you sure you want to do it in Jamaica, or are you just hype because we had damn oxtails for dinner?" They both burst into laughter.

"No, I really think it would be dope, we could have a beach ceremony like you said and then just party on the beach afterwards, I'm feeling that." Troy was in agreeance.

"Yay, I'm so excited! That was simple enough." They hi-fived and kissed.

"Now onto the next subject, my mother." Taylor paused.

Taylor and Morgan's mother had struggled with drug addiction their whole life. They never knew who their dad was, although it was rumored that their mother was the mistress of a well-known athlete who funded her drug habit for many years. Morgan always wanted to know who their dad was and especially if it was who they rumored it to be, but Taylor wasn't interested.

"So, what's your thoughts babe, and just so you know, I'm supporting whatever your decision is."

"I don't know. I haven't seen her in almost eight years, I mean we have talked here and there, but I just don't know if I want her to be a part of our day, she hasn't even met you before, and Morgan would probably have a fit. She's not interested in a relationship with her at all, whereas, I don't know what I want. I don't know, maybe the wedding is a bit much." Taylor was stressed.

"Look babe, don't stress yourself out about it, the wedding is over a year away, maybe make some attempts to get together before then and see how it goes before you invite her. Also remember it's your wedding not Morgan's. I know you want to make sure your sister is comfortable, but you have to do what you feel is best for you."

Taylor agreed with Troy and decided she would reach out to Cynthia Hayes soon to see if their relationship could be salvaged in time for her wedding. She loved that she could talk to Troy about anything comfortably, so it took her by surprise when he turned cold when she brought up starting a family.

"We've been talking about important matters all night, communicating without a problem, now all of a sudden you're so tired and ready for bed, it's barely nine o'clock, since when do you go to bed this early?" Taylor was upset.

"What's so frustrating about me asking when you thought we should start trying for a child? I'm not meaning at this moment babe, I'm not trying to be pregnant at our wedding especially not in Jamaica." Taylor laughed, but Troy said nothing.

"What is up Troy, talk to me, I deserve to have an answer." Taylor was serious.

"Fine, you want my answer, I don't want any children." Troy stood up and grabbed he and Taylor's plates from the table and placed them in the sink.

"What? Are you serious right now?" She was shocked.

"Very." Troy looked directly into her chestnut colored eyes that began to fill with tears.

"I guess this is a conversation that we should have had a long time ago, I just assumed that once we were married we would start a family, this changes a lot of shit." Taylor turned to walk away, Troy grabs her hand but she pulls away.

"What does it change? We love each other, that's all that matters."

"It's not all that matters. I want to be a mother, I want to raise a family together, be grandparents together one day. Don't you want to be a father?"

"My daughter died, I missed my chance to be a father." He snapped.

The tears were rolling down Taylor's face.

"Oh ok, I see what this is about. AGAIN. Everything that happened with you and your ex-wife haunts our relationship. So, because you experienced an unfortunate situation with losing your child, you make the decision that WE can't have children and you think that's fair?"

"Life ain't fair." Troy walks out of the kitchen and heads up the stairs.

Taylor took her last sip of wine as she walked into the living room grabbing a throw blanket and crawled on the couch, laid down and quietly cried herself to sleep.

Chapter 17

The next few weeks between Troy and Taylor were difficult. They each used work as a way to suppress feelings, so they barely saw each other. They didn't talk much, kiss, or make love. Taylor had even removed her engagement ring. Troy had noticed and was quite upset, but knew her reasoning and didn't want to restart the fire, so he said nothing.

Taylor hopped in her car after work with plans on stopping at the grocery store before heading home, but those plans changed when she received a call from Ms. Diane. She didn't sound well and asked if Taylor could come by her apartment. Taylor agreed and immediately called Troy.

"Hey what's up?" he answered.

That upset her. He always called her Tay or Baby and considering they hadn't talked much, she thought he would be excited to hear from her. She pushed her own feelings aside and explained that she was headed to his mom's house and that she would keep him updated once she got there. He thanked her, told her he would be on the way and said he loved her before hanging up.

Taylor cried the whole ride to Ms. Diane's place. She loved Troy wholeheartedly, but knew that with him not wanting children, the relationship would have to end. She knew that's how they both felt, especially since they had been avoiding each other, but felt they each were too afraid to say what needed to be said. She knew she had to find the strength to let go, but truly didn't want to.

When she arrived at Ms. Diane's she had a fever, headache, body aches and a horrible cough. Taylor suspected it was Covid, and it was confirmed once she had her take an at home test.

"I can't believe I went all this time not catching this damn virus and now we at the tail end of it now I'm sick. I know I shouldn't have gone over to Mae's house last week, she had too many people over there, that's probably where I got it from." She shook her head.

"Well, you just have to rest up now, I was going to the grocery store anyway, I'll pick you up some things and between Troy and I, we will come by to check on you, speaking of which, let me call him, he said he was going to head this way." She picked up her phone to call him.

"Yeah tell him don't come by here, it's bad enough you're in here, I don't want ya'll to get sick."

Taylor let him know what was going on with his mother and the plans to go to the store for her. They hung up and Taylor caught a glimpse of a side eye glare from Ms. Diane. She followed her eyes and realized she had noticed that she wasn't wearing her ring.

"Now what's going on here? Last week when Troy came by here, when I asked him where you were, he gave me some old dry answer and now today you're not wearing your engagement ring. Talk to me Taylor." Diane was concerned.

She sat up some in her queen-sized bed equipped with a floral sheet and quilt set. She adjusted her mask and placed her glasses on.

"Well the truth is, we are in a really rough space right now." Taylor became emotional.

"What happened, what is going on?" Diane was genuinely concerned.

Taylor wiped her tears and explained that they weren't on the same page regarding having children and that she didn't know if they would make it because having children was something that she really wanted.

Seeing Taylor upset, made Diane emotional. She really loved her, not even just for her son, as a person in general. She couldn't believe that her son had changed his stance on having children since Naomi had lost their child. She wanted to be a grandmother just as much as Taylor wanted to be a mom, but she also knew that Troy still had some issues from his previous marriage that were unresolved.

"I wish I could give you a hug, but know that I understand you. I know Troy may still have some issues with everything from his former marriage, but I know how much you two love one another. I mean ya'll just got engaged, got the house, and should be planning a wedding. I pray ya'll can work this out." Diane was serious.

"I do too, I love Troy and I know he loves me, but I don't want to force him into having children if it's not what he wants, it just won't work and that breaks my heart." Taylor walked to the bathroom to get herself together.

Diane was furious and as soon as Taylor left, she called Troy.

"Hey Mom, how you feeling, I'll swing by tomorrow to check on you, just make sure you have that mask up and plenty of Lysol." He laughed, but realized his mother was quiet.

"Ma, you there?' He asked.

"Yes, I'm here, just not in the mood for your jokes right now. Now what's this I hear about you not wanting children? Taylor running around here without her engagement ring on, ready to leave you." Diane didn't know how to ease into conversations, she got right to the point.

"Wait what, ready to leave me? That's what she said?" Troy asked.

Diane realized that she probably shouldn't have said anything, but it was too late and she needed them to get their act together. She sipped some water after a coughing episode and continued to tell Troy about the conversation she had with Taylor. Troy was upset. He couldn't believe that Taylor had talked to his mother about it and that his mother felt it was her place to mention it.

"With all due respect mom, right now both you and Taylor are out of pocket. Not only is she telling you she wants to leave without she and I even talking again about the issue, but you just feel comfortable confronting me about it and on top of it all neither one of ya'll thinking about my reasoning for not wanting kids. That whole experience was tough and I'm just not ready to go through that whole process again, I'm scared as all hell.

But ya'll don't see it from my point of view." Troy was heated.

"I do son, and I apologize for meddling, don't take this out on Taylor, she was just confiding in me, that's what us women do. I shouldn't have said anything, but I couldn't help it. Ever since you went through all you did with that Naomi, all I prayed for was someone that was good to my son, so now that you have that, I don't want you to lose it. Do you understand where I'm coming from?" She asked.

"I do mom, but please focus on getting better, and let Taylor and I figure this out. I'll see you tomorrow. Love you."

He hung up his phone and banged his hands on the steering wheel. His mind was racing and he had no clue how to remedy the situation.

Chapter 18

Troy walked into their home and looked around. He loved everything about it. The beautiful hardwood floors, the high ceilings and especially the way Taylor had decorated it. She took pride in their home and made sure it was up to par. But he knew that what his mother said was true, it was a strong possibility that it wouldn't be his home for much longer. They hadn't married yet and Troy's name wasn't on the deed, and even knowing that he still felt like he didn't want children.

He headed into the kitchen and sat his keys on the island. It smelled delicious in the home, he leaned over to look in the pot to see Taylor's infamous Italian sausage and peppers. He grabbed a spoon and scooped just enough out to get a taste. It was delicious, he couldn't wait to have a full serving. Just as he closed the pot, the patio door slid open.

"Look at you, always in the pots." Taylor smiled and shook her head.

"I couldn't resist, it smelled so good. Hey Tay how was your day?" He asked.

There was obvious tension between the two and they went on with the small talk for a few moments before Troy jumped into the issues.

"So, I see that you haven't been wearing your ring and mom told me that you said it's basically over because I said I don't want any children. Is that right?" He asked.

He caught Taylor off guard. She was used to Troy trying to avoid the difficult conversations that she was always open to have. She knew Diane would tell Troy what she said, she just wasn't expecting to have the conversation so soon.

"Well yeah, umm, I guess we are both at fault for not having this conversation prior to us getting serious, getting engaged and getting a home together, but I've always wanted to be a mom and I assumed you wanted to be a dad. I just can't put the thought of not being able to create a life, and raise a child together behind me. I've always been able to achieve everything I went after in life, my degree, my artwork, the man of my dreams, everything except motherhood." Taylor started to cry.

Troy started to feel weak. He truly loved Taylor and didn't like seeing her upset. He pulled the stool from under the island and sat down.

"You're right babe, we should have had these conversations beforehand but we were so busy enjoying each other, it never crossed our minds, so we're here now. My intention isn't to rob you of your dreams of being a mother at all. But you have to at least admit that you can understand where I'm coming from with this, with everything I went through losing my first."

"And I understand and can't imagine going through that, so yes, I do realize that it may be scary for you because your ex-wife wasn't able to complete the pregnancy, and I sympathize with you losing your child. But if I'm being honest, being scared due to what happened and not wanting a child are two completely different things. Shit,

I'm scared, 1 in every 5 women have miscarriages, let's not forget about the ones who have still born births, or even children with special needs, there's always a risk with having a baby. It hurts to know that you were so open and ready to have a child with someone who by your own account, wasn't good to you, but when it comes to me, you don't want to have kids by the one who you claim you love like no other and has been good to you from day one, make that shit make sense Troy." Taylor was upset and frustrated.

Troy stood up and wrapped his arms around Taylor. He understood what she meant completely and was realizing he was in fact scared versus actually not wanting children. He was excited when Naomi found out she was pregnant and devastated she lost the baby, and didn't want to go through that again. He also knew that Taylor would be a great mother and deeply desired it due to her not having her own mother by her side most of her life.

He held her tightly and kissed her forehead. He explained that he was scared and willing to start a family with Taylor, under the condition that they agreed to only one child and to wait at least one year after they were married to have time to enjoy their first year of marriage before they ventured into parenthood. Taylor agreed and cried tears of joy. Troy had one more request, so Taylor headed upstairs and grabbed her sparkly engagement ring. She handed it to Troy and he got done on one knee.

"Let's try this again, Taylor Renee Hayes do you promise to never take this ring off your damn finger and be my wife." They both laughed as she promised and allowed him to slide the ring on her finger.

Chapter 19

Taylor prepared herself to head to the inpatient facility that her mother was currently in. She hadn't seen her in years and only knew her recent whereabouts because one of her closest friends was a patient at her job a few months prior. They had spoken on the phone a few times, but this would be their first face to face meeting.

Troy supported her desire to meet with her mother, but not her sister. She had hoped that she would go with her, or at least speak with their mother on the phone, but Morgan wasn't ready. She resented their mother for her drug abuse and leaving them for years on end. As much as she wanted Morgan to be on board, she knew she couldn't force her.

She walked into the facility and signed in. She sat nervously in the waiting area watching other families talk and eat lunch with their loved ones. She heard a soft voice speak her name and turned to see her mother walking into the room. Her eyes immediately filled with tears as she stared at the petite fair skinned woman with short curly hair. She stood up and awkwardly hugged her mother. She smelled just as she remembered her, Egyptian Musk Oil, as if she had just got it from 52nd Street.

Cynthia Hayes was still beautiful, yet you could tell she had been through a lot. She had lost some weight since the last time Taylor had seen her and the short hair was completely different from the long tresses she had always had pulled back in a ponytail. She wiped tears from her eyes as they sat down.

"You're beautiful Taylor, Wow! and I am so very proud of you. You've always wanted to be a nurse and look at you, nursin'." The pair both smiled.

Taylor was reminded of not only her mother's beauty but her sense of humor. She was always fun and energetic and Taylor loved that about her. She hated that drugs had claimed her so many years ago and prayed that this time in rehab would be a different outcome.

"Thank You. You look great as well. How's this place been treating you?" Taylor asked.

"It's been pretty good, everyone here is nice, the food is good, which is always a plus." She laughs.

"So, for the most part, all is well. But enough about little ole' me, let me see that rock on your finger. I'm happy you found true love Taylor, you deserve it."

Taylor held up her hand for Cynthia to get a better look at her ring. She couldn't help but smile thinking about Troy and being able to marry the man of her dreams.

"Oh, he did a great job." Cynthia began to cry.

"This ring reminds me of the one Nate gave to me." She put her head down.

"You were married? I never knew that." Taylor asked.

"No, it wasn't an engagement ring, your daddy kept me fly honey. I didn't want for anything and regardless of the situation, he worshipped the ground his girls walked on. Your sister was four years old and you were about one year old, when he found out about my habit. Begged me to go to rehab and that you two would be fine with him and his wife while I was away, and I didn't go. Used the two of you as an excuse not go, saying that ya'll needed me, that another woman wasn't going to raise my daughters and that I could stop on my own." She shook her head with tears rolling down her eyes.

"And look at me, still an addict, and didn't do right by the very people I claimed needed me. The last day I saw him, I'll never forget, when I refused to get help, he was getting ready to go on a road trip, he told me that me not going to get help was the biggest mistake of my life and that when he returned he would be back to get his daughters. He never made it back from that road trip, He and a teammate went out after their game and got into a car accident in Portland. His teammate made it, he didn't."

Taylor couldn't help but cry as her mother wept. She reached out and grabbed her hand.

"I know it wasn't right, for he and I to even be together, Nate Harvey was a married man, but I loved him and he loved me, I know he did. His wife was good for his image, a good career, from a good family, and there was me, just a pretty light skin girl from West Philly. I ain't have shit going for me, I dated drug dealers until I met Nate, and the money he gave me was a gift and a curse. The weed led to cocaine, and when he died and I couldn't afford the cocaine anymore, it was crack."

Taylor was speechless, she had heard rumors of who her dad was, and about her mother's addiction, but to hear it straight from her mother was different. Although she was hurt that her mother wasn't in her life, her story helped her gain some clarity.

"How is Morgan, I would have loved to see her, but I know how she feels about me, all I can do is pray for her forgiveness."

"She's doing well and yes give her some time." Taylor knew Morgan's stance and respected it and didn't want to give Cynthia too much information on her.

"So how did we end up with Aunt Vanessa?" Taylor asked shyly.

Cynthia looked up as if she was shocked by the question. She stared at Taylor momentarily before she answered.

"Denise Harvey arranged that whole thing." She looked away.

"Who?" Taylor was clueless.

"Denise Harvey was your dad's wife, when he passed away, she arranged for your dad's sister, your Aunt Vanessa to care for you and Morgan. She bought the house in West Philly for Vanessa, paid all her bills, and provided everything for you and your sister."

"So, wait a minute, Aunt Vanessa wasn't your sister?" Taylor was confused.

"No ma'am, I only had one brother and he died when we were younger, you and your sister were raised by your paternal aunt."

"She knew everything about you, she had pictures and everything." Taylor exclaimed.

"I'm sure she did, she and I used to be the best of friends, we were the same age, that's how I met your dad. We drifted apart when I started getting high, that's how your dad found out. I resented her for that for years, when in all reality it was the best thing she could have done. She did a great job with my girls. And the affair that produced two daughters had to remain a secret, Denise didn't want anyone to know that he cheated and had two daughters. From what I heard, her plan was to say the two of you were adopted had your dad really been able to make good on the threat to take you and Morgan from me. But when he passed away to keep from raising you two alone, she had Vanessa do it."

Taylor didn't know how to feel. She was happy to finally know the truth, but conflicted to know it all as well. She felt sad to have never known her mother or father and wished the adults in her life had done better at being honest. She hugged Cynthia and was leaving more confused than she was before she arrived. She still didn't know if she would be inviting Cynthia to the wedding, or even talking to her again. She checked her phone as she got in her car to notice a text from Morgan asking her how it went. She couldn't wait to call her and fill her in.

Chapter 20

"So many things make so much sense now, everything about me seems much clearer. The type of men I date, how wild I was as a teenager, everything. Minus the drugs and I'm her." Morgan laid her head back on the sofa.

"Right, and I think for me, it's why I want to be a mother so bad, to be there, and support my child, be a part of everything in their lives, that's what I longed for, a mom and a dad to be there for me. Yeah, we had Aunt Vanessa, but there's nothing like a mom and a dad by your side."

Taylor walked over to her cabinet and pulled out two wine glasses.

"And that was weird as fuck too. I don't understand why we couldn't know who our dad was or that Aunt Vanessa was his sister that was raising us, that shit is baffling. Especially after he was already dead, what did it matter.?"

Morgan rolled her eyes and took a sip of the semi-sweet wine.

"From what she was telling me his wife didn't want people to know about us, it would mess up his image and legacy as well as tarnish their marriage. Aunt Vanessa got taken care of to keep quiet, she apparently would tell people we were her foster daughters."

"I know you fuckin' lyin'? Morgan couldn't believe it.

"Listen, I was floored listening to all of this. What's even crazier is mom was out here getting high living reckless and she outlived both Aunt Vanessa and the wife."

"Exactly, that's why you gotta live, shake a little ass, smoke a lil' grass, have good sex, and shop til' you drop."

Morgan held her wine glass up and started twerking. They both laughed and Taylor got emotional.

"What's wrong Tay?" Morgan was concerned.

"Please don't take this the wrong way Morg, but you remind me so much of her. I swear ya'll have the same personality, always knowing how to make someone laugh. I'm going to go see her in a couple of weeks, you should come." Taylor smiled.

"Come on now with that shit, you go visit this lady one damn time, ain't seen her since God knows when and now I act just like her, girl please. And furthermore, I'm not interested in going to see anyone who couldn't come to see us off for prom, graduation or any other activity we had"

Morgan was annoyed and didn't have a problem letting Taylor know.

"It's one thing for us to talk about the puzzle pieces of our lives, but for you to start trying to link me to someone who abandoned us when we were toddlers is insane. I love you to death and I'm not trying to have any drama or for anything or anyone to come between us, so do me a favor, moving forward don't talk about her to me, I'm not ever going to see her, because I truly don't give a fuck about her." Morgan was serious.

Taylor took a sip of her wine and tried to process everything that Morgan had just said to her and responded with two words.

"She's dying."

Chapter 21

Life was hectic for both Troy and Taylor. Solid Brick had become Troy's full-time job after he secured a bid with the city revitalizing properties for low income families. There were several contracting companies that would be working together over a three-year period, he was excited to be one of them. He and Naeem had put together a great team of guys and they all worked well together.

Between work and painting, Taylor was just as busy. She had been promoted to Shift Supervisor in the labor and delivery department at the hospital and had also launched her online art store. She painted in the evenings or on days off when she wasn't too exhausted.

Taylor and Morgan had gone through an awkward phase of communication after Taylor's initial visit and Morgan stating that she wasn't interested in being in communication with or updated on their mother's condition. Cynthia had full blown AIDS. Between the drug use and promiscuity, she had no idea how she contracted it twelve years prior, but she hadn't taken care of herself or taken her medications like she should have and it progressed from HIV to AIDS quickly. Taylor had respected Morgan's wishes to not update her, and made plans to cremate Cynthia whenever she made the transition.

She missed her sister and was looking forward to getting together later in the week for much needed drinks and to catch up. As much as she prayed that her sister would forgive their mother and visit her before she passed away, she knew it wasn't up to her and that she had to allow her to process everything on her own timing.

Taylor couldn't wait to get home and relax. She stopped on the way home to pick up Chinese that Troy had already ordered. She arrived home and called out for Troy, to no answer. She knew he was home because his car was in the driveway. She placed the food and her purse down on the island in the kitchen and headed upstairs. She called his name once more before walking in their bedroom.

Troy was sitting on the edge of the bed with air pods in scrolling intently through his phone. When he realized Taylor had walked in, it startled him causing him to drop his phone. He frantically picked it up and took the air pods out of his ear and quickly placed his phone in his pocket.

"Hey Tay, you scared the shit outta me. Did you see my text about the food?" He asked nervously.

"I did. It's downstairs. What's wrong though babe, you seem on edge or something." She noticed how quickly he put his phone away, but didn't want to jump to conclusions or be accusatory.

"Nah, I'm good. Just looking over some pricing and shit for this job, listening to crazy ass Wallo and Gillie on this Podcast. I ain't even hear you come in babe. How was your day?"

Troy stood up and kissed his fiancé on her lips. She smiled and wrapped her arms around him.

"Today was a day, but when isn't that the case at Lankenau, all I want is my spicy shrimp and broccoli, some wine and you." Taylor squeezed him a little harder and inhaled his freshly showered aroma before kissing him again.

Taylor got a quick shower before they headed down to eat.

"Can you believe in less than a year we will be husband and wife?" Taylor lifted her wine glass to toast with Troy.

"Yeah, I can absolutely believe it, in fact, I was just having this conversation with my mom about moving everything up." Troy looked up to see Taylor's reaction.

"Are you serious?" She was excited.

"I mean what exactly are we waiting for? You have your ring, we have the house, we may as well go down to the justice of the peace and get it done. You mean to tell me Diane Jennings didn't mention this at all to you?" Troy was shocked.

"No, she really didn't." Taylor laughed.

"So, you don't want to do Jamaica? I mean it doesn't matter to me at all, we can still honeymoon there, but city hall works fine with me." She was excited.

They held their glasses up again to toast to their upcoming nuptials.

"Babe, I can't believe it, that means Baby Jennings will be loading by 2023." She smiled from ear to ear.

Troy became a little irritated. Although they had agreed to wait a year after marriage and have one child, he felt as if that was all Taylor talked about. He honestly could wait three or four more years but didn't even want to talk about it. He really did love Taylor and wanted to be married. He wouldn't spoil the moment. They finished their bottle of wine and headed upstairs to enjoy one another.

Chapter 22

Taylor stood in their full- length mirror admiring her look for the night. Her black jeans fit her like a glove and the black blazer she wore with her burgundy Jeffrey Campbell cowboy boots completed her outfit perfectly. She wore a neat bun atop her head and did a natural make up look for dinner and drinks with her sister.

"You look good Tay, I have a serious question though." Troy stood behind her admiring her beauty.

"Yes babe, what's your question?' She smiled.

"You sure them titties ain't gonna pop out the blazer?" Troy smacked her butt.

"Oh my god, no they not, the blazer is specifically made to not wear a top under it crazy, ain't nobody gonna see ya babies." She laughed.

"Oh, ok just checking. Where ya'll going to eat at anyway?" He asked.

"Buddakhan, those lobster egg rolls are calling me." She answered.

"Oh yeah them jawns fire, bring me some home babe. And Naeem probably come by, we gone watch the game, and go over some shit for these upcoming projects."

"Ok, cool. Well I'm heading out, Morgan claims she's already on her way." She rolled her eyes.

"You know damn well that's a lie, Morg probably ain't even dressed yet."

They both laughed as he walked Taylor to the door to hop in her car.

To her surprise, Morgan had arrived and was standing at the bar. Her shoulder length bob was perfect and her make up was flawless. Taylor leaned in to hug and kiss her sister, as Morgan began to shake her shoulders side to side, causing her boobs to shake.

"Girl, what the hell." Taylor pulled back from the embrace laughing.

"Hey sister. Look at you, god damn, Morgan's lil' sister is bad." She lifted Taylor's arm and spun her around.

"Oh, my goodness, I'm going to be married with kids and still be referred to as your little sister."

"You damn right. "They both laughed.

"And what's this talk about kids, didn't you say Troy wasn't interested in having any?" She grabbed two lemon drops from the bar and passed one to her sister.

"Well that's why we needed to have dinner and catch up, a lot has been going on."

They headed to the hostess stand and waited momentarily until they were seated.

"So just like that he's okay with having a child and ya'll aren't having a wedding anymore, just going to city hall? I'm not feeling it. Well not the part about having a child, I'm excited for you, I know it's something you really want and I can't wait to be the rich auntie, but I am a little salty we won't be seeing ya'll get married in

Jamaica like the original plans." Morgan made a sad face and sipped her drink waiting to hear from her sister.

"Sister don't be sad, you'll be there when we wed as a witness, and we can all go out for drinks and dinner, we will surely celebrate."

"Yeah that's cool, I mean it won't be a Jamaica type celebration, but I guess." She smiled.

"Who all is the WE that will be there during the nuptials?" Morgan asked.

"The usual suspects, you, Ms. Diane, his partner Naeem, Ivory, and Cynthia." She spoke their mother's name softly and quickly lifted her drink to take a sip.

"And that is exactly why I asked, I had a feeling you were including her in your plans, and that shit is so annoying honestly Tay. I think it's very selfish of you to want me to feel the same way that you do." Morgan was upset.

"I'm not telling you how to feel or expect anything, I'm asking you as my sister to support my wishes for the day that I get married. You don't have to say two words to her, it's something that I want for my day, that's all. I don't even truly know how I feel about her, some days I'm with it, some days it's upsetting, but for the day that I say I do to Troy, I would like her to be there. For me, knowing how sick she is, and that I finally have contact with her, having her there is like closure for me, and that has nothing to do with you. I hope you understand that." She extended her hand across the table awaiting her sister to grab it.

Morgan took a bite of her Tuna spring roll, wiped her mouth with her handkerchief, smiled and grabbed her sister's hand.

"I wouldn't miss your day for the world, just don't expect too much from me regarding her, this is for you." She was serious.

"Speaking of favors, you know the guy on the Nets I told you about that I've been talking to. Well, his agent, who is actually from here, has a new business venture, he's opening an upscale jazz club here in a few months."

Taylor was confused as to what she had to do with any of that.

"I'm really trying to lock this one in Tay, I really like him." She smiled.

"So, my question is, what does that have to do with me? All you have to do is stay interested in someone for more than two weeks." She laughed.

"I know, you know I get bored easily, but not with him, I really enjoy his company. He's different. I kind of told him that I manage you." She squinted her face and awaited her sister's reaction.

"What? Manage what crazy?" She shook her head and smiled at the same time.

"We were at dinner and his agent was talking about the décor for the restaurant and how he wanted it to be filled with black art, so I kind of brought you up. Davon isn't like other guys I've dealt with, he prefers substance, and you know, I haven't had a job or any desire to work since

I've dated the type of men I've dated, but honestly, I want to be the one for someone one day and have my own love story like you and Troy. So, I ran with the story that I managed your art career and was working on an exhibit for you, and getting your art noticed. Davon makes me want to do more with myself, no one has ever made me feel that way."

"Morg look at you blushing, you must really like him, but I still don't get what I have to do with it. You've already told them you're my manager, what do they want a reference check?" Taylor laughs.

"Sort of, his agent, Tommy Kirkland, wants to meet with the artist, so that would be you, and I told him I would arrange it."

"You are something else. You are lucky I love you. When does he want to meet with us?" Taylor asked.

"Well see, that's the thing, he already knows me, he wants to have a meeting with the artist to get a better understanding of the work and to see if it fits the vibe and aura. I told you it's different with Davon. Outside of Tommy being his agent they are good friends and are really into knowing people on spiritual levels and all that, the first athlete that I have ever dated that was this deep."

"So not only do I have to meet with him, I have to do it alone, Morgan, you wild for this. I'm only doing this because you didn't give me too much grief about Cynthia being there when Troy and I marry. Set up the damn meeting and let me know when it is." She playfully rolled her eyes at her sister.

Morgan smiled and pulled her phone out to email Tommy to start the process of setting up the meeting. She sat her phone down, and the two enjoyed the rest of their night together.

Chapter 23

Troy was awakened by the alert on his phone at almost two in the morning. He reached up for his phone and panicked. He dropped it on the floor causing Taylor to change directions in her sleep. He waited a few moments to know that she was still asleep, then he picked up his phone and crept out of the bed.

He hurried downstairs into the living room to read what appeared to be an email from Naomi. He sat up for almost two hours reading the three sentences over and over again. He didn't know how to feel and wasn't sure that it was even her but he had to know. The last sentence ripped at his heart, seeing her type that she still loved him knowing he would soon be married to someone else.

A part of him wanted to erase the message and any memory of Naomi, she had hurt him deep and left him with no explanation. The other part of him wanted the explanation and to know she was safe. As much as he hated to admit it, he still loved Naomi. He paced back in forth in the living room contemplating whether to respond or not. The urge inside of him would not die, he hit send on the email, telling her that he loved her too. He plopped down on the couch and exhaled deeply. He leaned his head back and eventually dosed off to sleep.

He was awakened by Taylor climbing on him on the couch, gently kissing his neck.

"How'd you end up out here baby?" he asked as she gently massaged his head.

He gently grabbed her waist and began to rub her back causing her to lay her head on his chest. Troy caressed her back with one hand while he reached for his phone with the other, checking to see if Naomi had emailed him back and also being sure nothing was in plain sight for Taylor to see.

"I was hot as hell in the room last night and came down to get something to drink and ended up falling asleep down here. You ain't even notice I was gone, the way you were snoring." He squeezed her butt causing her to jump up.

"Babe stop, and I do not snore." She laughed.

"Yes, the fuck you do, if I don't fall asleep before you, it's a wrap for me."

"Whatever Troy Jennings, you ain't never complain about me snoring before, so I don't believe you. You were probably out here chattin' with chicks on social media." She smiled and playfully gripped his neck before kissing him.

Troy tensed up. Although he wasn't on social media, he knew Taylor would be pissed to know he was emailing Naomi in the middle of the night. He had to change the subject so she wouldn't pick up on how nervous he was.

"I'm a just record ya ass snoring next time so you know it's real. But in the meantime, I need about ten minutes of your time." He gently kissed her on her neck and stood up, she wrapped her legs around his waist. He carried her to the kitchen counter and laid her across it.

He buried his face between her legs and pleased his soon to be wife while he fought thoughts about his ex.

Two weeks later, Troy and Taylor exchanged vows at City Hall. Simple and sweet with the people they loved the most present. It warmed Taylor's heart to now have a picture with her husband, sister, mother in law and her very own mother. Morgan kept her promise to attend despite Cynthia being there, and went beyond expectations by speaking to her and even giving her a hug. Taylor stood in awe looking on at her loved ones, while Troy stood admiring his new wife.

She looked flawless in an off shoulder fitted, fish tail style dress. It accentuated her curves, and her long curls fell perfectly on her back. Diane had requested a picture of the new couple in front of the infamous LOVE statue in Center City, so Troy walked over to his wife to oblige to his mother's request. The wind blew gently on the chilly March day, so Troy removed his perfectly tailored navy-blue blazer and wrapped it around his wife. The natural smiles and expressions of the newlyweds due to the oversized blazer covering a majority of her petite frame made for beautiful pictures.

The newlyweds and their guests headed to an intimate dinner at Butcher and Singer to continue the celebration. The next day Mr. and Mrs. Jennings boarded a flight to enjoy a last-minute honeymoon to Mexico.

Chapter 24

The married life suited the Jennings' well. They both worked hard, yet always found time for one another and did things to make life easier on the other. The transition from boyfriend and girlfriend to husband and wife was painless for them.

The warm May breeze on the drive home from work inspired Taylor to light the grill once she arrived at home. She multitasked on their patio, putting the final touches on a painting that she simply titled "Love", while the chicken breasts on the grill cooked to perfection. She took a sip of her favorite red wine before she reached for her ringing cell phone.

"Mrs. Jennings speaking." She answered and smiled.

"Well hello there Mrs. Jennings, I heard you had the grill rolling." Diane laughed.

"Yes, I do, and there's plenty of chicken and I made a salad, are you coming by to keep me company since that son of yours is working late again tonight? I can call you an Uber." She asked.

"Well I can call my own Uber, thank you very much." She laughed.

"Look at you Momma Diane, with your own Uber account."

"Yes, since Troy insisted on getting me the Iphone, he downloaded a bunch of mess to it, Uber, Cash App, and Instagram, speaking of which you ain't accepted my request to follow you." She jokingly snapped.

"Instagram? I'm hollerin'. I have so many requests, hold on one second let me see. Is this you? LadyDi8659? You gotta put a picture up Momma, so people know it's you." She laughed.

"Well you can help me do all that when I get there, listen I have a couple pounds of shrimp I don't want to go bad, I'll bring them and we can throw them on the grill, steam them or whatever. I'll call my Uber shortly and see you in a little bit." Diane hung up and gathered her belongings.

The two sat and enjoyed their meal, the beautiful breeze and conversation for over two hours before Troy arrived home. He was exhausted as he talked about some complications he and Naeem had run into on their current project. Taylor made his plate and poured him a glass of wine while he tried to relax.

"These issues with the plumbing are going to set us back and we have another job set to start, running out of manpower, these niggas don't want to work these days, after that covid shit and all that unemployment and PPP money, people are lazy as hell and we actually pay well. Naeem said he has a guy that may work out, so hopefully it does, these late nights are killing me." He shook his head.

"Me too, we've barely seen each other all week." Taylor pouted.

"Well, everything will work out son. Ms. Gladys son, Corey, you remember him, right? I know he was looking for work, you want me to give him your number? Diane asked.

Troy was now sidetracked, a notification from Naomi had popped up on his email. He quickly closed the notification and sat his phone down on the table face down. Taylor noticed, but didn't say anything. She stood up from the table and went to reach for Troy's plate.

"Hold up babe, I was going to ask for a little more chicken if you don't mind. And yeah mom, give him the work phone number, I think he specializes in flooring and carpets, so that would be really helpful." He sipped his wine and thanked his wife for adding more to his plate.

Taylor was visibly irritated, and began washing the dishes and putting food away. Troy sensed it and walked up behind her as she washed dishes and kissed her neck. She gently pushed him back and told him to stop. Troy looked around to see if his mother noticed, and she hadn't. She had made her way to the living room and was busy on her phone.

"What's up babe? I can't hug on my wife?" He asked.

"You tell me what's up Troy? Between the late nights, you always in your phone, and what was that tonight at the table, putting your phone face down, that's some new shit." She spoke firmly but in a low tone, as to not alarm Diane.

"I just explained why my nights are longer and always in my phone? Who isn't these days, everything is done on our phones." He turns and looks at his mother.

"Look at her, on her phone. Come on now Tay, don't start overthinking shit and creating scenarios in your damn head." He looked at her in the eyes.

"Look Troy, I don't know, but it's just felt weird lately, and listen I could be wrong, but you know for sure I'm always going to say how I feel." Taylor stared at Troy.

"I know that and it's one of the reasons I love you, so straight forward and honest, but I'm telling you, you have nothing to worry about. Give me a minute to get the staff right for these projects, and we will get back to our regularly scheduled program. I promise you." He kissed her forehead and then her lips.

"You promise?" She whispered.

"I promise. Now what we doing for dessert, we ain't got no cookie dough or nothing?" he asked.

"I mean what's sweeter than me?" Taylor laughed.

Diane walked into the kitchen as the two shared a sweet kiss.

"Look at you two. I love to see it. But what I would love to see even more is my bed. Let me pack up some of this food for my lunch tomorrow and be on my way." She grabbed a container out of the cabinet.

"Mom it's almost ten o'clock, no one is driving you home this time of night after all the wine we've drank and you're not getting in an Uber either. You might as well head on upstairs and pick a room." Troy gave his mom a hug.

"Are you sure, I don't want to be a bother."

"We have our own room; how would you be a bother? Ma'am head on up and go lay down. I have some brand-new pajamas you can slip into to get comfortable, I'll bring them up you." Taylor replied.

"Alrighty then, I'm gonna head up, it's way past my bed time. Good night." Diane hugged them both and headed up the stairs.

"Babe, I'm gonna grab a shower, really quick, I'll be right back down to help you with the kitchen."

"Don't worry about it, there isn't much to do, go get your shower, I'll meet you in the bedroom." Taylor winked and smacked Troy's butt.

He shook his head and went upstairs to get a shower.

While in the bathroom, Troy pulled out his phone to finally read the email from Naomi. He locked the bathroom door to be sure Taylor didn't just barge in. If Troy had any complaint about Taylor, it was the lack of privacy at times. She didn't care if he was in the shower or on the toilet, she had no issue inviting herself in.

Naomi's emails were getting longer and longer, and each time she expressed how much she loved and missed Troy. He was in too deep. Each day he hoped to see an email pop up from her, at times weeks would pass before she would respond, but each time she did, Troy responded as soon as he could.

This time was no different, he told her that he loved her and that he needed to hear her voice and talk to her. He demanded the truth about why she left and told her there were some things about his life he needed to tell her as well, but would only share on a phone conversation. He needed to know if it was in fact Naomi. He also needed to let her know about Taylor. He loved her, but knew that his feelings for Naomi would always interfere with their marriage until it was resolved one way or another.

Chapter 25

The grand opening of Art and Soul had arrived and Taylor couldn't wait to see her art displayed. Tommy had selected a total of three paintings to help decorate the newest, most talked about restaurant and jazz lounge in the city. There was set to be a huge media presence as well as well- known sports and entertainment industry folks. Although Taylor was excited, she was also a little upset that Troy would be late to the event due to work.

"I'm not saying I don't understand, because I do, but, I can still be disappointed. This is huge for me and I wanted you to be there." Taylor explained as she stood in their walk-in closet checking out her outfit.

"I'll be there at 9 no later than 9:30 Tay. We should be done here around 8:30. The site is about ten minutes from Naeem's crib, I have my clothes with me, I'll shoot there, hop in the shower and be on my way. But you get there, smile and do your thing. See you later baby. Love you."

"I love you too." Taylor hit end and tossed her phone on the bed.

She stood in the mirror turning side to side making sure she looked just right. She had splurged on a black Rasario lace off the shoulder dress for the night. She felt it was the perfect mix of art and fashion for the evening. She opted for soft curls that her stylist pushed to one side and adorned with a beautiful hair pin that matched her dress. The all black look popped perfectly with the beautiful red lip and smoky eye makeup that she wore.

She sprayed herself with her Bitter Peach perfume and headed downstairs.

Taylor prayed as she walked to the black 2022 Escalade that waited for her in the driveway. The driver opened the door and helped the 5'2" beauty climb into the truck. They pulled off and Taylor smiled as she was excited for so many people to see her work.

As they arrived she became nervous. There were so many people lined up to get in, and so much commotion as the red carpet was laid out and celebrities were taking pictures and talking to the media. Tommy had pulled all the stops to ensure that the grand opening was a success and from the looks of it, that would absolutely be the case. She noticed Morgan on the red carpet with Davon and decided she was ready to get out. The driver opened her door and she gracefully walked past onlookers feeling amazing. A hand grabbed hers and gently pulled her through the crowd.

"You look absolutely stunning." Tommy whispered in Taylor's ear.

She smiled and graciously followed his hand-held lead through to the red carpet. He extended his arm and motioned for her to pose for the camera. Taylor felt like a celebrity, she smiled and posed for the cameras all while hearing her sister cheer her on. After a few turns and twists, she walked over to her Morgan where the two embraced.

"Sister, you look absolutely stunning. "Morgan squealed.

"Thank you, and you look gorgeous as well, this look is giving very much outer space and out of these girls league."

Morgan hi-fived her sister and spun around in her Zhivago metallic gold mini dress.

"Thank you, sis, but where's my brother in law." She looked around to see if he was in tow.

"Girl, he got caught up at work, he won't be here until about 9:30." She rolled her eyes.

"Oh, that shit could have waited, this is a huge night for you, but whatever, you better head over, Tommy is trying to get your attention."

Taylor walked over and stood next to Tommy, who introduced all five of the artists whose work would be displayed. She smiled brightly as he said her name and highlighted that she was the only woman who had work displayed in the restaurant. He held her hand up and kissed it gently with his full lips. Tommy was attractive and he knew it. He was tall, well dressed and had all the gentleman like qualities that women gushed over. His salt and pepper hair and beard complimented his perfectly fitted navy blue suit and million-dollar smile.

   Taylor posed for pictures with the other artists, and other key people of the restaurant before heading indoors. She couldn't wait to see not only the restaurant but her work. The live band played an upbeat jazz selection as patrons began to flow into the restaurant. Art & Soul was dimly lit and had a beautiful grand piano at the entrance. Behind the piano there was a spotlight against the wall and Taylor noticed one of her paintings. She smiled and fanned her face to try and stop the tears from falling from her face. Although she had hosted her own art show, having her work displayed for so many strangers to see was surreal. The gold and black abstract painting fit the décor perfectly. She traveled through the restaurant and admired everything from the elaborate bar set up to the raised stage in the front of the club, everything about Art & Soul was exquisite.

Taylor took her reserved seat at the table with Morgan, Davon, and another couple. Troy's seat was empty and Tommy didn't have a date. Taylor pulled out her phone and texted Troy to see how long he would be as it was already past 9 o'clock. He quickly responded that he would be there shortly. The restaurant was to capacity and the band had everyone grooving to the sounds. The restaurant staff brought out delicious appetizers and cocktails while they enjoyed the ambience.

Tommy was very attentive to Taylor, causing a photographer to assume they were a couple. As Troy arrived at the table, the photographer took multiple pictures of Tommy and Taylor.

"Beautiful couple, these pictures are flawless." The photographer said as she worked the room snapping pictures of everyone.

Troy cleared his throat, and reached his hand out for Tommy and introduced himself as Taylor's husband.

"Nice to meet you sir, I borrowed your wife for a minute, she made my pictures look good." Tommy let out a hearty laugh that wasn't too well received by Troy.

Taylor noticed the awkwardness and stood up to greet her husband. She kissed him and introduced him to everyone at the table. They sat down and Tommy tried to ease the obvious tension in the room.

"So, Troy, I hear you are a very skilled contractor. I may have an upcoming project for your company, I'll be sure to get your contact info before the night is over." He picked up his glass of cognac and took a sip.

Troy nodded, but clearly was not interested in doing any business with Tommy. They dined, drank and enjoyed the restaurant until almost 11 o'clock before they headed home. The ride home was quiet but once they arrived, they both had a lot to say.

"You never once congratulated me, asked to see where my work was in the restaurant, nothing and I truly feel a way about it Troy." Taylor took her shoes off grabbed the remote to turn the television on in the living room.

"I never got a chance to, I was excited when I got there until I get to the table and you taking pictures and shit like that was your husband with the nigga." Troy snapped.

"Please, I knew you were going to go there. I mean no one would have had to assume anything had you been there, everything gets put on hold for work."

The segment of the news covering the grand opening had just started, they both turned to the television. They showed Tommy as the restaurant owner and showed pictures and footage from the opening. The broadcast showed the portion in which Tommy held up Taylor's hand and kissed it and it triggered him. He thought of the day he arrived at Naomi's job to see a man doing that very thing to her and then her disappearance.

"Well would you look at this shit. Besides the posing for pictures and him "borrowing" my fuckin' wife, your ass letting him kiss all on you, what the fuck is that Taylor Jennings, did you forget you're married?" Troy paced the living room floor.

"Don't say kiss all on me like he tongued my damn mouth down Troy. He's way older than me, that's what older men do, kiss women's hands. I wasn't the only woman's hand he kissed tonight, what the fuck is the big deal." She snapped.

"The big deal is, you're the only one that made the news lookin' like his woman, the only one in all the pictures with his ass, again lookin' like his woman, and it is a big deal. What your naïve ass views as just a kiss on the hand is how wives end off runnin' the fuck off."

"So not only are we name calling, because apparently, I'm naïve, you're really just triggered yet again by your ex-wife. This isn't about me, it's about Naomi's ass and you know what, I'm quite tired of your outbursts and having to relive that bullshit ass marriage ya'll had."

Taylor walked off and headed up the steps to their bedroom. She slammed the door shut which was followed by Troy pulling the television off the wall.

Chapter 26

Taylor pulled up to Starbucks and ordered her usual, a Grande Strawberry Acai Lemonade as she chatted on the phone with Ivory before heading to work.

"All jokes aside Tay, it sounds like ya'll need some therapy. I completely get where you're coming from, you know I do, but Troy isn't just your boyfriend or even your fiancé anymore, he's your husband. Ya'll have to try and work through this." Ivory was serious.

"I feel you, and I love my husband, but I'm not about to keep being on the end of his anger over somebody the fuck else. I've been nothing but good to him, I don't deserve to be treated like I'm the one who walked out on him, if he wasn't over her ass, he should have never proposed to me. It was his idea to push the wedding up not mine." Taylor was upset and had started to cry.

"Don't cry girlfriend. Troy loves you, I know he does, but I do agree, he still has some unresolved issues with that ex, but to be honest that's normal. He just needs to be upfront and address the elephant in the room so that ya'll can move forward. That's why I said ya'll should try and go to therapy. Trust me, it helped me so much when Keith and I broke up, and again when my dad passed away. You never realize how much baggage you're carrying around. Don't give up on your love is all I'm saying. I can send you a few good therapists I know and you take it from there, sounds good? Ivory asked.

"It does, thank you for hearing me out, I love you girl." She responded.

"I love you too and of course, you know how we do. Now let me get my ass back to work before I'm back in therapy for losing my damn job."

They both laughed before they hung up. As she pulled into the parking garage at work, her cell phone rang. It was Diane. Taylor rolled her eyes and forwarded the call to voicemail. She loved her mother in law, but she was so predictable. Anytime something happened, she called to make a million excuses for Troy's behavior and somehow blamed everything on Naomi, ranting about how much she disliked her and how she was nothing like Taylor. She didn't want to hear it, she just wanted Troy to get his shit together.

Taylor's work day was long and draining. All she could think about was her husband and how she wanted them to last forever. She pulled out her phone and texted Troy to tell him they needed to talk when she got home. He liked the text and she pushed through the rest of her work day, anticipating talking to her husband.

Normally, her ride home from work would consist of a good 90's R&B playlist and making stops to pick up whatever was in the plans for dinner. This day, she was only focused on getting home and getting her marriage back on track. When she arrived, Troy was already home, installing a new television on the wall in the living room.

"Hey, I went a grabbed a new tv, I'm almost finished putting it up." Troy hoped that his wife would forgive him.

Taylor wasn't impressed and wasted no time getting down to business.

"You could have left the wall blank for all I care, to hell with the tv Troy, what's up with us?" She asked sternly.

"What do you mean, you're asking what's up with us like we're some fuckin' high school couple. We're married, we had an argument, I overreacted, I'm correcting the shit and apologizing for my actions. Grown man shit." He leaned over to try and hug his wife, but she pulled back.

"No Troy, it's not that simple. First off, that apology was wack as fuck, you're not truly sorry, you're going through the motions of an apology, just to shut me up and I'm not cool with that. You have some real issues regarding your ex and how everything went down with ya'll and it's not fair to me to have to keep reliving shit that I wasn't a part of, I'm tired of it. Every time something happens you find a way to make it relative to you and her, and on top of that, the tantrums, breaking tv's and shit, it's just not right."

"So, you don't remember stomping up the steps and slamming our bedroom door, only what I did right, ok cool." Troy returned back to the area where he was installing the television.

"Really, out of everything I just said, all you remember is me bringing up you breaking the tv, and your response is to talk about me slamming a door as if I didn't have a reason? That's weird and lame as shit Troy and you know it. "Taylor started to cry.

"And you know what makes it even worse is that I know everything, not just your outbursts about her, but I know you've been emailing with her all times of the night, telling her you love and miss her and I STILL tried to make this shit work. But I can't do it anymore, as much as I love you, I'll never be Naomi and I won't sit and compete for your love with a bitch that walked out on you that is now your fuckin' pen pal."

Taylor removed her rings from her finger and placed them on the coffee table, picked up her purse and walked out the door. Troy stood in silence as she backed out of the driveway and sped off.

He called her repeatedly to no avail. After almost a half hour, she texted him and told him that she was at her sister's place and that she loved him but she needed space. As upset as he was, he had to respect it. That was more than Naomi had done years ago when she up and left. He couldn't believe that he was in the situation he was, on the verge of losing the woman who had been everything to him, to the one who walked away without a word. But still, he loved Naomi and couldn't quite shake her and he didn't know why. They emailed for hours that night until Troy finally asked where she was, she never responded after that, he fell asleep confused and angry.

Chapter 27

It had been almost two weeks and Taylor was still staying at Morgan's Center City condo. She missed Troy, but was still very uneasy about his unresolved feelings for Naomi. Morgan had just got back into town, she had been in Miami with Davon.

"Helllooooo." She sang out as she walked through her front door, designer shopping bags in tow.

"Sister Sister." Taylor sang.

She came out of the bedroom and practically ran to her big sister. Morgan sat her bags down and opened her arms widely to embrace her sister. They hugged for almost two minutes as Morgan rubbed Taylor's back as she sobbed.

"I know Tay, everything is going to be alright. I promise you it will. Troy knows what he has, and I know the situation with his ex-wife is a lot, but pray on it, give it time, and do like Ivory said, go to therapy. He also needs to cut the damn communication with the bitch, the emailing has to stop if he wants this to work." Morgan grabbed two wine glasses and looked through the wine fridge for the perfect bottle to pop open.

"White or red baby girl?" She asked.

Taylor began to cry again.

"Tay what's wrong, did Troy say he didn't want to work it out, what's up, talk to me." She walked towards her sister.

"Morgan, I'm pregnant." She sobbed as she looked over at her sister.

"Oh my god, are you serious, I'm going to be an aunt, I can't believe it! Come here, give me a hug." She hugged her sister who continued to cry and never lifted her arms to hug her back. She lifted her head and gently wiped her tears for her sister.

"I just can't believe this and as much as I want to be a mother, this is just the absolute wrong time. I don't even know if my marriage is going to last and here I am pregnant." Taylor shook her head.

"Ok first of all, stop being negative, no one's relationship is perfect, you and Troy have some shit to figure out, but this baby is a blessing, a blessing that you've been dreaming of." Morgan reached out for Taylor's hand.

"I know, I just had this whole vision in my head about how it would be when I found out I we were pregnant and it was nothing like I envisioned. I was here, alone, at my sister's house, no wedding ring on, haven't talked to my husband in over twenty-four hours, you weren't even here, I just feel so lost." Taylor placed her hands over her face and shook her head.

Morgan hugged her sister once more and grabbed her a bottle of water and remembered she had brought her a piece of cheesecake from their favorite bakery.

"This is like heaven, it's no way this cheesecake should be this good." Taylor smiled as she licked the fork.

"So damn good, and it has tasted the exact same for years. But wait, you never told me what Troy's response to the news was like." Morgan grabbed a fork and scooped up some of the delicious pineapple cheesecake.

"I haven't told him." Taylor never looked up and continued eating.

"WHAT? Taylor, I know you lying?" Morgan put her fork down and waited for her sister's response.

"I just don't know what to say. We planned on waiting a while after we got married, I don't know how he will react, you know considering the circumstances regarding his first child and we are in such a weird space right now, you know?" She asked.

"No, I don't know. This is not you, you've always been the most upfront and willing to talk things through person I've known in my life. I mean me keeping a secret, or running from a difficult conversation okay, but not you. You have to tell him, regardless of anything, that is your husband and this is his child. I understand there's a lot going on, past and present, but he should know about this Tay." Morgan was sincere.

"You're right, I guess I have to put my big girl panties on, I can't believe there is a baby growing inside of me, I truly don't know how to feel." Taylor explained.

"Me either, I'm so excited and don't worry, you'll be a natural at this, just like everything else. I got your back baby girl. I love you, well ya'll." Morgan smiled and hi-fived her sister.

"We love you too Auntie Morg."

"So, while we're talking about important shit, I have some news to share as well." Morgan said.

Taylor smiled and moved her eyes towards her belly and Morgan noticed her.

"Hell no, did you forget I was just offering you wine? I am good on being an auntie, I don't know about the whole have a baby of my own thing. But no, I spoke with Cynthia yesterday for hours on the phone and as difficult as part of the conversation got at some points, it was so easy, refreshing and fun at others." Morgan smiled.

"Really Morg? Wow! I don't even know what to say. I mean I am happy for both of you, but I also understand it's not all lollipops and rainbows. After our initial conversation, I felt the same way. A part of me happy to see her and be in her presence, seeing her bright personality, but also still a little hurt and full of questions, so I completely understand that. She called me yesterday too, but I had just taken the pregnancy test and my mind was all over the place, I never called her back."

"Yeah, she was probably calling to tell you that we had talked, typical mom stuff I guess. As soon as they talk to one child, they gotta call the other." They both laughed but Morgan quickly becomes serious.

"Her health is concerning me, and the place she's in doesn't seem to be too attentive, she said the food is disgusting, and I even heard one of the aides not being very nice in the background while we were on the phone." Morgan seemed sad.

"When I spoke to her last week they were having sloppy joe's for dinner like it's high school, and I was at work doing a double otherwise I would have taken her something else." Taylor shook her head.

"Just disgusting. But with that being said, I've been thinking about her all day and I think I'm going to have her come stay with me. I know it sounds crazy and I was so against even talking to her but that is our mom, and even though growing up without her was hard and even finding out about Aunt Vanessa and our dad has been mind boggling, I still just want to make sure she's okay and comfortable during this time. Basketball season is starting in a couple of months Davon will be busy with work, and I'll be home more often. Especially since I'm really getting serious about doing public relations and event curation now. Since I told Davon and Tommy that I was working with you, they've put me in contact with so many people, I'm working on a launch event for this jewelry designer from New York now, it's so much fun and lucrative might I add." She laughed.

"I'm getting all off topic, but the point is, what do you think about that?" She sipped her wine.

"Well first off, I am so excited for you with your new career. It's so fitting for you Morgan, you are going to do extremely well with this business venture. One thing about Morgan Lydia Hayes, she's going to create her own lane, I love it! And as far as Cynthia, I support you wholeheartedly if that's what you want to do, and I will also help out as much as I can when I'm not working or painting. We can develop a system so that it's not all on you. I commend you for opening up your home for our mom, it means a lot." The two hugged and continued to talk and plan out the next steps in both of their lives.

Chapter 28

Taylor pulled up to their home and was instantly annoyed. Troy's truck and a mysterious car were in their driveway causing her to have to park on the street. It wasn't even noon on a Sunday so whomever was there for sure had spent the night. Her day off that she had planned to return home and try and figure out their marriage was starting off bad. She immediately thought of Naomi. Taylor thought to pull off, but remembered what Morgan had said just a couple days prior, some conversations regardless of how difficult they are, had to be held. She opened har car door and walked swiftly up to her home. She took a deep breath, placed her key in the door and turned the lock.

The smell of bacon filled her nose and made her nauseous, she couldn't believe that whoever was there had the nerve to be cooking breakfast in her kitchen. She didn't make it to the kitchen however, she had to pit stop at the half bathroom to vomit. As she leaned over the toilet, Troy called out her name and began walking towards the bathroom.

"Tay, what's wrong?" Troy asked as he stood at the door.

Taylor flushed the toilet, washed her hands and rinsed her mouth before she told Troy they needed to talk. As she walked out of the bathroom she walked towards the kitchen to see who was parked in her driveway and making breakfast in her kitchen. Troy walked slowly behind her. She was surprised to see Ms. Diane in the kitchen cooking.

"Good morning Taylor, I'm so happy to see you, I prayed on it last night, I promise you I did, God answers all prayers." Diane walked towards her to give her a hug.

Diane knew they would need time to themselves, so she let them know that once she was finished she would be heading home. She asked Taylor if she noticed her car in the driveway. She had finally decided to get back on the road after years of not driving due to an accident she had many years previously. Taylor felt crazy to believe that another woman had been staying at her house, and in that moment knew she had to make her marriage work. She knew Troy still had some kind of feelings for the woman that had left him without a word, but also knew that their bond and love for one another trumped that.

As she sat in the kitchen chatting and waiting for her mother in law to finish breakfast so she and Troy could talk, she admired her husband as he pulled plates and glasses down from the cabinet. He noticed her watching him, smiled and mouthed that he loved her, while Diane went on and on about her car and driving again. Out of nowhere again Taylor was nauseous and hopped up to run to the bathroom, but didn't make it. She had thrown up in the hallway and it didn't take long for Troy and Diane to realize what the issue was.

"When I say the lord answers prayers, I mean he answers prayers. Lord have mercy, thank you Jesus! I can't believe I'm going to be a grandmother." Diane threw her hands in the air and watched as Troy and Taylor hugged and cried.

"So how do you feel?" Taylor wiped her eyes and looked up at Troy.

"I feel good, happy you're here and shocked but I'm ok, nervous but I'm ready. How do you feel is the bigger question, have you been sick like this every day?" Troy asked.

"No, like I said I took the test two days ago, only because my period was a few days late, this is the first time this happened to me, it hit me when I walked in and smelled the bacon." She answered.

"Let me open up some windows, clear that smell out for you, I wonder will you even be able to eat the bacon." Diane moved swiftly opening windows and even lit a candle.

"Well we gonna see, I sure am hungry." Taylor laughed.

They sat down to eat breakfast and Taylor had no issues finishing her breakfast including the bacon. Shortly after breakfast Diane said her goodbyes and hopped in her Honda Accord and headed home. The Jennings knew they had a lot to hash out and wasted no time getting to it. They talked for almost two hours about everything from therapy to Naomi.

They agreed that they would seek couples' therapy and make their marriage a priority which included Troy promising to not work late two days a week. They wanted to spend as much time as possible to prepare for how different things would be once the baby arrived.

Troy admitted what Taylor had already known about him being in communication with Naomi. He said that although he knew how bad she hurt him by leaving, there was never any closure and he always wondered where she went and what made her leave without just ending the marriage. He talked about how he could never trust her again and did not love her in the manner that he loved Taylor. He felt comforted in knowing that she was in fact alive and would cut communication with her and be open about it once they started therapy so that he could move completely past it. She was thankful for his admissions and felt comfortable knowing that they were committed to making their marriage work and to becoming parents. They showered and spent the day in bed making love and resting.

Chapter 29

The pregnancy and therapy were going well. It was New Year's Eve and Taylor was almost four months pregnant. They were hosting a small party at their house and Taylor was in the kitchen making appetizers for the night.

"Babe did you get the avocados so I can make the guac?" Taylor asked.

"Yeah, they should be right over there, next to the sink. You see them?" He yelled from the living room.

"Ok I see them thank you, in a few minutes I'm going to need you to run and pick up the desserts from the bakery."

"I already asked mom to pick them up so I could stay here and finish helping you out, she actually should be here soon, she made some seafood dip for tonight. And oh yeah, if Morg is going out of town with Davon, what is Ms. Cynthia doing tonight?" Troy asked as he used the Swiffer to clean the hardwood floors.

"I meant to tell you, I asked her if she wanted to come over and she said she would let me know if she was feeling up to it, so I'll call her in a little bit to see how she feels and if so, I'll get her an Uber so we don't have to leave out. Naeem and Kira are picking up the wings, we have all our liquor, the desserts are handled so yeah, we're all good." She opened the fridge and placed the guacamole that she had just made in the refrigerator.

Troy came into the kitchen and walked up behind his wife and kissed her neck and then slid his hands around her waist to her belly and gently caressed it. Taylor leaned her head back and enjoyed the caress, but it reminded Troy of Naomi, when he would rub her belly, he moved his hands up and focused on her breasts instead. Therapy was helping, but he still struggled at times with thoughts of Naomi.

"I'm just realizing I'm steady yelling we have all our liquor and I won't be having one sip tonight." She playfully pouted her lips and crossed her arms, Troy laughed.

"Oh, Shit I forgot all about it, not even a sip of your favorite wine. But it's all good, I'll have Kira whip you up something non-alcoholic, and just think in five months, you'll be ready for the real thing." He kissed her forehead.

"Yeah let me text her now and tell her to be prepared to hook me up a cute lil' drink. And unfortunately, I won't be drinking in five months, remember I'm breastfeeding babe." She shook her head and grabbed a bottle of water.

"Yeah that's right, but it's no big deal, how about this, after tonight, I'll stop drinking as well, I need to cut it out anyway, I'm over here looking like I'm the pregnant one." Troy laughed as he patted his belly.

"They do say dads gain that pregnancy weigh too, I like you a lil' thick baby." She licked her lips and softly grabbed his manhood.

They kissed while walking slowly towards the living room. Troy walked backwards and gently fell back on the couch. Taylor climbed on top of him and kissed his neck gently.

"Mrs. Jennings, I like where this is headed, but if you ever call me thick again it's gonna be a problem." They both burst into laughter before they made time for a quickie on the couch.

A few hours later, everyone was in attendance enjoying good food and music waiting for the ball to drop and 2023 to begin. Taylor danced as she enjoyed her non-alcoholic lemon drop martini as Kira and Ivory sipped on the real thing. Troy was in a heated debate with Naeem and their friend Jordan about football and Ms. Diane drank a glass of wine while sitting on the couch watching the Rockin' Eve television special.

As Taylor rubbed her belly and danced to the music her cell phone rang. It was Cynthia, so she assumed she was feeling better and ready to head over. She was wrong, she could barely talk and said she needed help. Troy and Taylor, rushed over to Morgan's apartment, where they found Cynthia passed out on the kitchen floor unconscious. They immediately called 911, and she was rushed to Jefferson hospital.

Once at the hospital she was placed on a ventilator due to respiratory failure, a complication from the AIDS virus she was infected with. Taylor called Morgan whose flight wouldn't arrive until early the next morning. Taylor prayed their mother would make it. As the clock struck twelve, Troy hugged and kissed his wife while they stood in the waiting room. Taylor began to cry and grabbed her stomach. Troy became nervous.

"Babe what's wrong, sit down." He grabbed her hand and walked her towards the chair.

"I'm ok, I just felt the baby kick for the first time." She held her hand on her belly as the tears rolled down her face. Troy placed his hand, but could not feel anything. He hugged his wife and gently caressed her back. They sat down and drifted in and out of uncomfortable sleep throughout night in the waiting room. Morgan arrived at about 7 a.m. and was in distress. She and Taylor talked and hugged and sat nervously waiting to hear anything.

Taylor convinced Troy to head home and get some rest under the condition that by noon she would be heading home herself and that Morgan would remain om duty. They embraced and he gently kissed her on the forehead and rubbed her belly. Once he was home, he took a long hot shower and laid across their California king bed. He called his wife to see if there were any updates and to tell her that he loved her. He tossed and turned in silence trying to fall asleep. As soon as he began to drift off, a notification alert from his phone startled him. It was Naomi she had finally responded to his last email. He had promised his wife over and over again that he was done with caring about Naomi. He talked about it week after week at therapy and he just knew that if she ever reached out again he would have the will power to ignore her. He didn't. He was still weak for Naomi despite his love for Taylor. She had finally explained everything that

Troy wanted to know, and although she had hurt him deeply, she was now in danger and he had to help her.

Chapter 30

Collectively, Morgan and Taylor decided to have their mother removed from the ventilator. Her kidneys and liver were failing and there was nothing more the doctors could do. Her daughters were by her side as she took her last breath just seven hours after she was removed from the ventilator. Troy picked them up from the hospital once they had said their final goodbyes. The car ride was quiet. Morgan sat straight up with her sun sunglasses on and Taylor was sleep. They arrived at the Jennings' home and headed in. Morgan helped herself to a drink at their bar while Troy held Taylor tightly gently rubbing her hair. He didn't know what to say, the relationship between Taylor, Morgan and their mother was odd and a bit awkward at times, but he knew that he had to be supportive.

Taylor grabbed a banana and sat at their kitchen table holding back tears.

"It's like, I don't even really know how to feel. As thankful as I am to have had the time that we did, I almost feel like, I would have rather not, if I knew the time would be this short, especially as I am embarking on this journey of motherhood. I just pray I will be a good mom." She rubbed her belly.

"Babe cut it out, you're going to be a great mom, don't you start taking on the shortcomings of others and making them your own. You made peace with everything with your mom, and that's that. Ya'll are two different people." Troy looked directly in her eyes while talked.

"Both of ya'll are so right, I don't know how to feel either and you are not Cynthia Hayes, you're going to be a great mother. I know one thing for sure, I'm not in the mood for a funeral. I wish we could just privately say our goodbyes and close this chapter out." Morgan threw back a shot of tequila.

"We can. She's not married and has no other kids that we know of, so we can do what we want. I feel the same way Morg. We can have her cremated and have a small memorial service with us, our closest friends, and her one good friend Ms. Sylvia." Taylor looked over at Morgan for approval.

"When do you think the memorial service will be?" Troy asked nervously.

"Well the hospital says they will release her body in about two to three days, so in the meantime, we can figure out who will cremate her and where we can have the memorial at." Morgan replied.

Taylor noticed how anxious Troy was and wondered what was going on.

"Babe, you ok? You seem like your mind is elsewhere." She waited intently for a response.

"Yeah, I'm good, just a lot going on with your mom's death and this potential project in Florida. we're trying to solidify." Troy lied.

"What project in Florida.? You didn't mention it." Taylor inquired.

"I didn't get a chance to with everything going on, plus Naeem and I have to get some paperwork in order to even be able to be a part of it. Basically, one of the guys from the city that we work with on the housing development projects, has a line on something similar that's about to start in Florida. Because we're licensed here though, it's a bunch of red tape and paperwork to do, but it's worth it. It's a lot of money involved. So, we trying to take trip to get everything in order and meet with some of the head honchos down there." Troy opened the refrigerator and grabbed a beer.

"That's great news, the timing just sucks." Taylor let out a huge sigh.

"I am exhausted, I just want to shower and take a nap. You staying here Morg?" She asked.

"Yes, I am, if ya'll don't mind, I can't go to my place right now, especially not by myself." She held her head down and grabbed her face. Taylor came over and gave her a hug.

Troy went out to pick up take out for Taylor and Morgan before he headed over to Naeem's house to talk about the lie he had just told his wife.

"Nigga, first off, why are you going anywhere for Naomi? I really don't fuckin get it. Fuck when she left you, you just got out the dog house with your pregnant wife about this same person, now you're going to rescue her and you put me and our business the fuck in it. I'm tell you now, this ain't gonna end well. I can feel it. You know Kira and Taylor talk and consider each other friends now, so when you leave and I'm still the fuck home then what. This shit don't even make no sense. Leaving your pregnant wife at home for a bitch that left you for fuckin' dead." Naeem shook his head.

Troy knew his plan wasn't the best, but he had to try and help Naomi. She had explained in her email that she was initially intrigued by David Randall, he was handsome, charming and a millionaire. She was infatuated with his lifestyle and as they slipped deeper in debt after she lost the baby, she was curious. She had agreed to go on a date with David and had the time of her life. They went shopping, dined at a five-star restaurant, and had amazing conversation about everything under the sun. They went to his place and ended up having sex, afterwards they made plans to be together and drank and had more sex. She started to feel sick and not like herself, she was dizzy and felt nauseous and eventually passed out. When she woke up, she didn't know where she was at the time, but it became evident that she was set up by David and was now a slave to a sex trafficking network. She apologized to him for even going on a date with David and the hurt she had caused him, but told him that she never stopped loving him and missed him. She begged him to help her. She had befriended a native older woman from Columbia who was the housekeeper where Naomi and the other women lived and worked from. The villa in Cartagena was beautiful, it served as a tourist attraction to the naked eye, but everyone including the authorities knew behind the closed doors what went on. Constanza wanted to help Naomi and all of the women there. Her family was well known in Columbia and although for many years she knew what was going on, she had grown weary of the crimes that surrounded her family. She was paid well to keep the villas clean and her mouth shut, but with a recent diagnosis of a terminal illnesses, she had nothing to lose by helping Naomi or any of the other women that wanted to be helped. Troy would book a villa that included Naomi and with Constanza's help, leave with his ex-wife.

"So, let's say Taylor buys the story that you're going to Florida to handle some business, ok cool, you go to Columbia, and bring back Naomi to do the fuck what? You're married and have a baby on the way with your wife. You know the one who ain't never turn her back on you." Naeem was pissed.

"I'm not expecting you to understand my reasoning, I don't think anyone will, that's not what I'm asking of you. If I could just forget about Naomi, I would have done that shit years ago. I don't know what the fuck is gonna happen when we get back, shit for all I know, me just helping her out of this fucked up situation could be all to it. We could get back and I never feel the need to talk to her again, just knowing she's safe and not in harm's way could be enough for me. I just don't know and I'm never going to be able to shake her until I face this shit." Troy leaned back on Naeem's couch.

Naeem still wasn't feeling the idea but knew Troy was hell bent on going, so they perfected the lie as much as they could and moved forward with the plan. The day after the memorial for Cynthia, Troy was on his way to Columbia to save his first love.

Chapter 31

Troy told lie after lie to his wife regarding his whereabouts and what he was doing. He knew she deserved the truth but knew it would break her heart again. He knew that if she found out, he would lose her forever and that if he didn't try and help Naomi, it would burn inside of him forever. He was in a lose- lose situation and just prayed for the best. He boarded the plane, texting Taylor that he loved her and emailed Naomi and Constanza that he was on the way.

He slept the entire flight and felt nervous and weak as he headed off the plane. As Constanza explained, there was a driver waiting for him at the airport. He called to talk to Taylor, lying yet again telling her that he had just arrived in Florida and would call once he got settled into his hotel room.

The ride to the villas was almost an hour and he was anxious. As he arrived, he knew instantly who Constanza was. She was a petite woman with long dark hair and evil eyes. He felt uneasy as he exited the car, wondering had he made a mistake. It was too late though, he took a deep breath and walked into the villa. Constanza made herself busy, but was sure to keep her eyes on Troy. Before long, he was headed to his room.

The villa was beautiful, if not for what went on there, it would for sure be somewhere luxurious to visit. The marble white floors, beautiful architecture and old Hollywood themed furniture, were breathtaking. He opened the door to his room and peeked in. He eventually walked completely through the door. There were candles lit and light music playing. The beautiful white curtains moved in sync as the warm breeze blew through the large windows. Just as Troy walked over to the window to see the view, Naomi called his name.

Troy was almost too nervous to turn around, but he did. She stood there as beautiful as he remembered her. Her eyes filled with tears as Troy walked towards her. He reached his arms out and pulled her in. They both cried as they hugged. The hug led to a passionate kiss that was interrupted by the room door opening. In the doorway stood a man who quickly shut the door behind him. He began talking in Spanish and walking towards Troy and Naomi. She dropped to her knees and begged for the man to stop, but it was too late, he had pulled out a gun and pointed it at Troy.

Troy was frozen, there was nothing he could do and despite Naomi's pleas, he pulled the trigger.

Troy sat straight up in the bed, sweat dripping profusely. He looked around his bedroom wondering how he ended up there. It wasn't the villa or the bedroom he shared with Taylor. It was the bedroom of the home he shared with Naomi. He was dazed and confused when he heard Naomi's voice. She stood over their bed and spoke softly.

"Babe we need to talk. I'm sorry about how I've acted recently, you were so right. I've been so stressed and hurt and being back at work has been hard as hell. I really want our marriage to work, I love you. Let's figure it out, for us."

"Sometimes our minds take us to unknown places beyond our wildest dreams. Proof that reality and imagination are closely related and at times co-exist."

- Aaliyah Shalawn

Follow me on IG:
@aaliyahshalawn
@wmn_thebrand

Made in the USA
Columbia, SC
20 June 2025